torilakesfreedmanthegodmoie@gmail.com

Author House

A-Our
COLLECTION
of
Everybody Stories
Storieyz
by Tori Lakes-Freedman
finally shipping out Sept. 12, 2019
Moie, Sissey, Momma, Fred, female dog,
RIP, Tootsie, "Hey" Victoria, little sister,
Torila, Ralph,
THE GODMOIE
Loves All ye (y'all) a whole Mess !!

authorHOUSE

AuthorHouse™
1663 Liberty Drive
Bloomington, IN 47403
www.authorhouse.com
Phone: 1 (800) 839-8640

Published by AuthorHouse 11/13/2019

ISBN: 978-1-7283-3574-2 (sc)
ISBN: 978-1-7283-3573-5 (e)

Library of Congress Control Number: 2019918582

Print information available on the last page.

TO: Michael Kelly → age 18 1967 vietnam

Finday Ohio – The Most Fun   June
                                                              1948 – ☒
        The is d̶x̶ Dedicated to my   2017
guardian Angel: DAVID L̶E̶E̶   Jan
                       DAY & Sheldon
                            & TOMMY
                                 & Nikki

To: John William Ward → From your gut

        take that and again Punching
               ↑   ↑   Bag

TO: 1976 Tour → Blacks & Jews with
    Harry Belafonte, who shaved my
life & Heather and Kellie, as well

    KoKo, MANGo, Vanilla, Sir
        stund ford   my son   Houston columbus
                                         by
1976   WAY of Kent
Patty Cake   1976   Park Zoo
Central Park CAROLINE   'Howletts'
    to   Central PaRk
Columbus

Firstly Deadicated

to

Mr. & Mrs Williams
of Avondale, Ohio

AND THEIR
offspring

KATT
WIALLIAMS

He made
me smile & makes
me smile. When
all of my
friends* and
family*
neglected
me in ~~1~~ 2016
to this moment
Sept. 11, 2019

* Not Diane Ellen Harris Bohana   * AND when convient:
                                     Tamol/vivi Kimora Baelett

Scottsdale Emergency units for picking up Rowbear more times than I can count.

For taking Rowbear and The Lady & Little Girl to Scottsdale Osborn Hospital

Mesa Fire & Police Dept.
↓
Scott Wilkins
Gilbert Police & Fire depts.

Police in Brentwood New Hampshire

N.Y.P.D. en MASSE

& Non-emergency (for He)
↓
NOT
=
I
S
O
D
E
M
A
N

3

-APPLICATION-

Title

Title of Work: A Collection of Everybody Stories

Completion/Publication

Year of Completion: 2017

Author

- **Author:** Tori Lakes Freedman
  Author Created: text
  Work made for hire: No
  Citizen of: United States
  Year Born: 1948

Copyright Claimant

Copyright Claimant: Tori Lakes Freedman
P.O. Box 2269, Gilbert, AZ, 85299, United States

Certification

Name: Joyce Santos
Date: April 24, 2017
Applicant's Tracking Number: 47858768

Registration #:   *-APPLICATION-*
Service Request #:   1-4965840511

Mail Certificate

Tori Lakes Freedman
P.O. Box 2269
Gilbert, AZ 85299 United States

Priority: Routine   **Application Date:** April 24, 2017

Correspondent

Name: Victoria Freedman
Email: arranger99@cox.net
Telephone: (480)539-3999
Address: P.O. Box 2269
Gilbert, AZ 85299 United States

4/21/17
Your LegalZoom Order # 47858768
Dear Victoria

Thank you for your Federal Copyright Registration through LegalZoom.

During review of your file, we noticed an issue that may delay the processing of your order.

On the application the author name is listed as **Tori Lakes Freedman.** We would like to know should we update the name of the author to: **Victoria Lakes Freedman?** That is the only issue that we have. Please advise on you would like to proceed.

Please feel free to contact our Customer Care Team if we can be of further assistance. Simply reply to this email, or call us toll free at (800) 773-0888. Our Customer Care Team business hours are Monday–Friday from 6 a.m.–7 p.m. PT

****

My response to the above e-mail, same day.

Re: Your LegalZoom Order # 47858768
[ref:_00DG0BmQx._5000f1C6UUQ:ref]

Thanks for the question.
The author of the collection, including all stories, is Tori Lakes Freedman. That should remain the author's name throughout all proceedings.

Can I assume that the copyrighting process will now be able to progress smoothly?
Please keep us posted.

Thanks again,
Robert M. Freedman
****

Victoria Freedman
P.O. Box 2269
Gilbert, AZ 85299

Order # 47858768

Dear Victoria:

Congratulations! Your application for copyright registration for "A Collection of Everybody Stories" has been submitted electronically to the U.S. Copyright Office. A copy of the application is enclosed for your records. Also included is a copy of the UPS Tracking receipt confirming that your deposit materials were successfully delivered to the U.S. Copyright Office.

Please Note: Your materials are not registered until you receive a certificate of registration and registration number from the U.S. Copyright Office indicating that the work has been registered. The time the U.S. Copyright Office requires to process an application varies and can take months. If your work is determined to be copyrightable and meets all legal and procedural requirements for registration, the U.S. Copyright Office will send the registration certificate to the individual or organization listed under "Mail Certificate" in your application.

If you have any questions or would like additional information, please call us at (800) 773-0888 Monday–Friday from 5AM–7PM and Saturday from 7AM–4PM PT, or you can email us at customercare@legalzoom.com.

We appreciate you choosing LegalZoom and look forward to serving you again soon.

Sincerely,

The LegalZoom Team

521527215

9900 Spectrum Dr.
Austin, TX 78717   tel 877.773.0888   legalzoom.com

Chp. 1

"Help, help," I yelled out to anyone who could.
No one was there so I kept running.

"Mom, mom, are you there," I screamed this time.
Suddenly someone grabbed me. I screamed so my throat hurt.

"Sshh," they whispered so I could barely hear them, "its ok,
Aja, Mom is here."

"Mom, I can't believe you are here," I beamed, "where's
dad?"

"They captured him, but don't worry I am here," she
managed to say without crying.

"What, we have to get him back, kill them off or something,"
this time I started crying.

" I know, but right now you and I have to be strong," she
pushed.

She tugged my arm and we hid by a bush.
I watched in horror as a herd of white men passed us.
They had at least twenty men and women tied up.
"What are they going to do to them," I asked afraid for the answer.

"Sadly, they will torture them," she answered, "make them
do all the work".

By then I had had it. I was not standing for this. So I ran out
in front of them and yelled, " you are evil men, you do not belong
on this earth. Stop doing this. We are normal people to. Just stop!"

"And *who* are you," this biggest man said.

"I am Aja, I am only 5 so you cant take me. HA!"
I felt so strong and alive.

"Do you have a mother boy?"

" Yes, but you demons took my father."

"Well, I think we should meet your mother, how about it?"

"Ok"

I tugged my mother out.

"Do you have a name Ms.?"

"Abbo," my mother said.

"Well Abbo I think it is about time to go"

And with that they put rope around my mothers neck, and took her away.

"Mom, Mom," but she was gone along with the rest. I could never forgive myself. I was to blame. I have been so stupid. I have to stop them.

Chp. 2

I screamed my mothers name. No one came so I ran around our village. No one was there so once again I kept running. Suddenly I came to an abrupt stop. A saw a white skinny man in front of me. Before I could think he grabbed me. He started running, so I did the only thing I could think of.

"You let me GO!" Then I bit him on the arm and stomped on his foot.

He dropped me to the ground. That still felt better than him grabbing me. I hid behind a bush until he ran away.
Who knew a white man could be a cowered. I thought thy were just thick skinned. When he ran I followed him to a ship. Not knowing what to do I boarded the ship. Seemed simple enough. Although I didn't realize I might meet my fate, right then and there.

I saw thousands of people: Woman, Men, even children and babies. that's when it occurred to me that they *could* take me. Even though the ship had not left it looked as though they had been on there for years. Some were already dead, some dying. The ones I knew were not that skinny, but they were now. They were tied up, even shackled. They were bleeding which boggled my mind. What had they done? Did they fight back, fall, or were already tortured? I knew one thing, I had to save them.

1st DAY OF 4th GRADE

11

This book belongs
to you. Mark, draw, write, tell
your blues, your smiles, your
own "Tyler" says: (up) ya got to stand up
star straight
arm down to you,
side, shoulders
relaxed

SAID when
asked how he felt on AGT

I AM
PROUD OF
Myself.

I AM alive
because of
MY SON
(since January 2017)
thank you Merrilee

IRVING Jesuse Diaz

A.K.A.

IRVIN GARCIA SR.

MARIA, MARIA, she tells it like it is, RowbeaR
the muscle of the family

Eileen: too gorguoes for MAMA & Papa good

IRVIN GARCIA JR.

Christopher — with his granddaddys EYES

Momma, I'll See You
In the morning you're
Chair is plugged up.
MY Head hurts I'm going
to bed Brooke is going
to watch victoria for
Me tonight call me when
you get home! Love
You very much!!! and
Thank you for being a
wonderful momma!!!
love, BOBBY

Ireland by way of Salisbury Mass. - Castle grounds
Sept ?, 1984 (Chezzy's B'day was celebrated: probably Kellie's Also.

Howetts Park Zoo or Howetts Zoo Park = Mr. Howletts had eye lashes
pulled out by one of his friends = they shared an apartment
in Kent, England = SIR; later he moved
to the Columbus Zoo W/ Patty Cake whom I met
at the Central Park Zoo and Auntie Caroline or Carolyn.
Cincinnati Zoo Gorilla area = lots of days over years.

The MARVelous Cee - Cee (my name for him.)

He started my Great Gorilla Adventure.

He Met Vanilla in Houston, Texas. San Diego Wild Animal Park, A very
MOMMA with her baby grasping Momma's left forearm as she sat on the
Momma's Palm. The one at the end of arm not the tree.

Member of the Gorilla Foundation from ≈ 1977 until I could not afford
to donate. Studied = ASL = to communicate with gorillas and other primates
My son, MANGO, capuchin monkey.

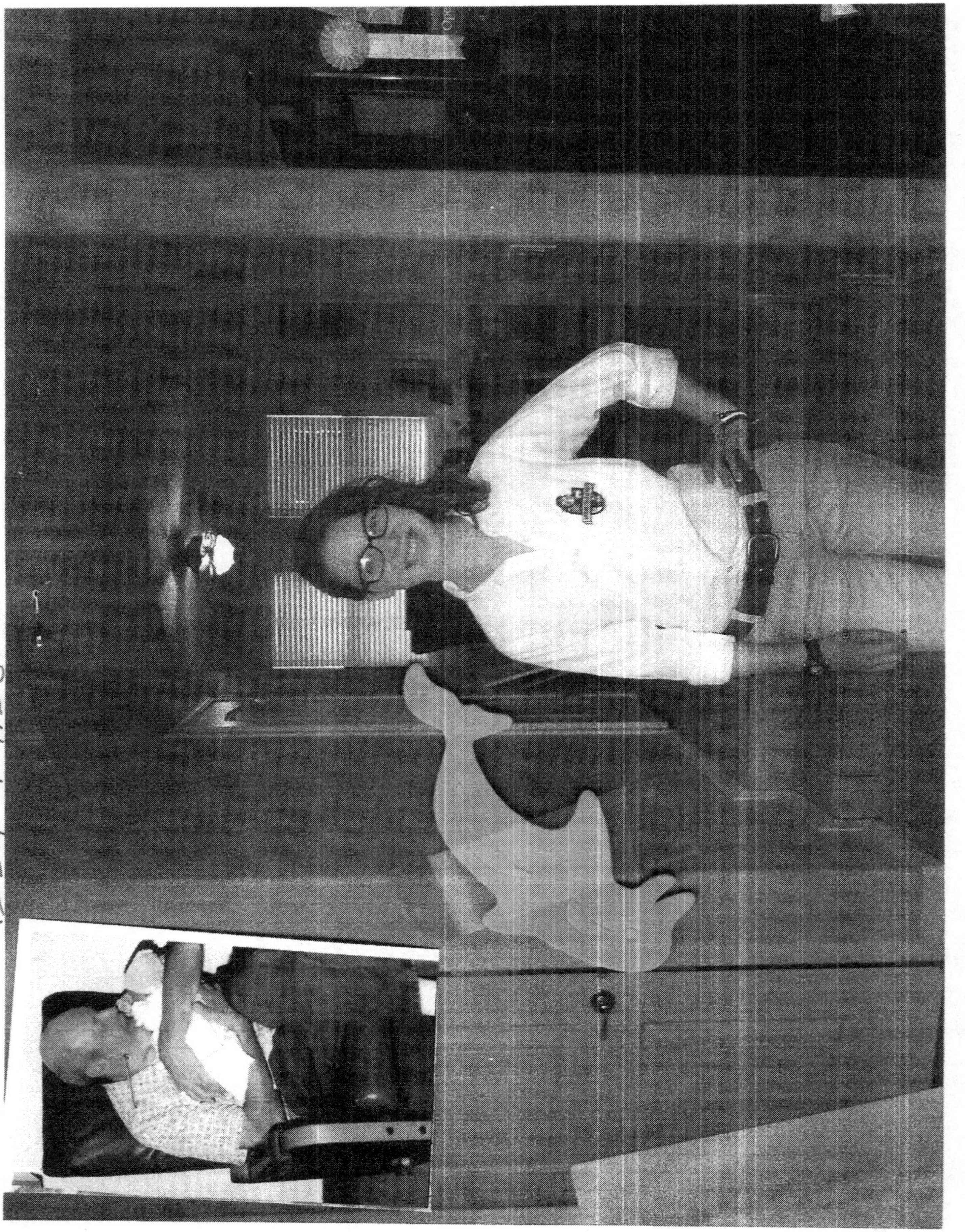

1st DAY OF 11th GRADE

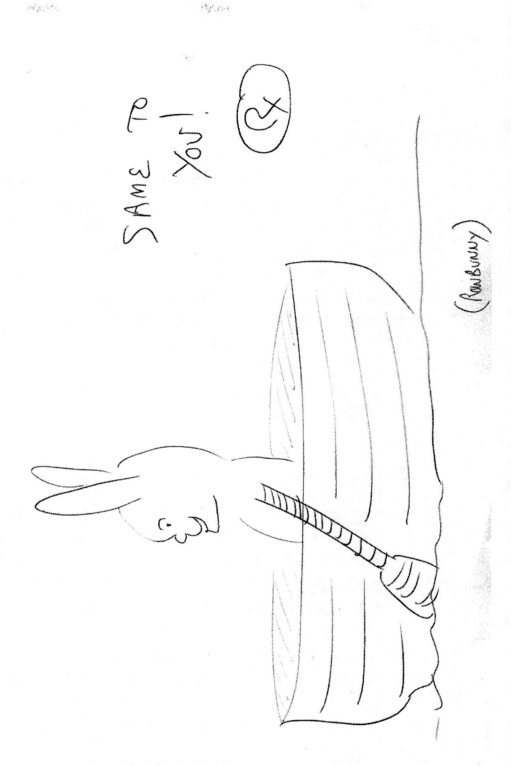

GABBIE'S COD ARTICLE

From funding the American Revolution into luring fishermen to the area, cod has been a crucial to the history, economy, and culture of New England. In the past three decades fisheries and government officials have noticed a significant decline in Cod populations, and have attempted to prevent further declines. However, a recent study headed by Andrew Pershing of Gulf of Maine Research Institute, proves that climate change and fisheries mismanagement are causes of this severe decrease in stocks. This study used data from Cape Cod all the way up to Canadian, Nova Scotia and was published in *Science Journal* as the first scientific report to confirm that climate change is responsible for less cod. In order to truly grasp the cause and effects of warming seas on cod, one must understand their lifestyle and the oceanography of the Gulf of Maine. The Gulf of Maine is in the Atlantic

Gulf Stream Current

encompassing lower parts of Canada down to Massachusetts, and is home to an ecosystem of marine fish and mammals that have adapted to very cold ocean temperatures. A prime fishing ground located 60 miles offshore, Georges Bank, is renowned by fisherman for producing massive numbers of cod; however, cod is scarce there as well. The Gulf Stream current is part of the deep-ocean current system known as the Global Conveyor Belt. Warm water, devoid of many nutrients, is carried along the Gulf Stream from Florida up to the Northeast where it is cooled by cold, dense water brought down from the poles, thus creating a frigid ocean climate that is teeming with nutrients.

In the Gulf of Maine the ocean temperatures have risen 4 degrees Fahrenheit, which is a sharper temperature increase than what was experienced in 99% of other major bodies of water worldwide. The study found that the cooling of the Gulf Stream now occurs further North due to changes in other major ocean currents in Atlantic and

Pacific waters. Cod thrive surrounded by cold water because it is both nutrient and Oxygen rich, but warming seas are pushing their populations to the breaking point. Fisheries officials estimate that cod populations in New England have decreased by 90% in the past three decades. The scientific study proves that an increase in warm water in the Gulf of Maine has not only decreased the number of new Cod but also decreased chances of fish surviving into adulthood – a deadly combination for a struggling species. Climate change has crafted a perfect storm for the cod as their food sources have moved Northward following the cool water, while predator populations, such as marine mammals, have bloomed making cod's centuries old home much less hospitable,

What is being done to save the cod? NOAA scientists have tracked cod populations for years in an effort to understand how the population changes and how to limit fisherman in order to preserve the species. However, this new study contradicts fisheries management decisions by claiming that, "The government has been overestimating the cod population and underestimating their mortality rates." The quotas set by the government have allowed overfishing because of the miscalculation of cod in the Gulf of Maine, as current stocks are only 3% of what can sustain a healthy population. John Bullard, regional NOAA administrator, says that he is not surprised at these findings and that, "management decisions made five years ago were wrong," because faulty models were all they had to guide them. Instead of purely surveying cod, as NOAA has been, the study suggest that researchers take a more "ecosystem-based" approach. The study's leader believes that federal officials need to take into account temperature, climate forecasts, food availability, and reproductive rates, "to provide a more realistic picture of the potential size of fish stocks."

Now that it has become clear that previous models developed by NOAA government officials falsely represent the actual number of cod in New England, scientists and fisheries management must come together to create a better management plan for this key species. Quotas have been continuously lowered over the years, but scientists believe that this is not enough to revive the populations. Scientists believe that they need to increase the number of areas that are completely off-limits to fishing because it will allow larval fish survival, reproduction, and an overall safe haven for populations to eat, grow, and thrive. The major obstacle officials and scientists face is the approval of new, stricter regulations by the New England Fishery Management Council. The executive director of the council agrees that they need to change their management tactics in order to cope with the threat of climate change and increased declines in fish stocks. However, many fisherman on the council do not believe that cod populations are in jeopardy, instead they say, "the study is entirely based upon the false premise that cod are actually at a low level." The extensive study proves that compared to historical numbers, cod populations are very low. Fisherman may say this because cod are easier to catch as their numbers drop because it forces them to congregate near popular spawning areas, as a natural response. Fisherman need to support an increase in the number of off-limits areas because without it the cod population is at risk to die out completely leaving them jobless.

Cod is incredibly important to the people of the Northeast, which is why they should support further protections of cod because it is possibly the only way populations will continue to survive. Overfishing, in part allowed by false government cod calculations has greatly decreased cod. In addition, the warming of the Gulf Stream and Gulf of Maine has forced prey to move Northward, and contributed to increased stress and mortality rates. Climate change coupled with overfishing has spelled disaster for this popular fish species, however if we act now the iconic cod can continue swimming and prosper once again in the waters of New England.

Pacific waters. Cod thrive surrounded by cold water because it is both nutrient and Oxygen rich, but warming seas are pushing their populations to the breaking point. Fisheries officials estimate that cod populations in New England have decreased by 90% in the past three decades. The scientific study proves that an increase in warm water in the Gulf of Maine has not only decreased the number of new Cod but also decreased chances of fish surviving into adulthood – a deadly combination for a struggling species. Climate change has crafted a perfect storm for the cod as their food sources have moved Northward following the cool water, while predator populations, such as marine mammals, have bloomed making cod's centuries old home much less hospitable,

What is being done to save the cod? NOAA scientists have tracked cod populations for years in an effort to understand how the population changes and how to limit fisherman in order to preserve the species. However, this new study contradicts fisheries management decisions by claiming that, "The government has been overestimating the cod population and underestimating their mortality rates." The quotas set by the government have allowed overfishing because of the miscalculation of cod in the Gulf of Maine, as current stocks are only 3% of what can sustain a healthy population. John Bullard, regional NOAA administrator, says that he is not surprised at these findings and that, "management decisions made five years ago were wrong," because faulty models were all they had to guide them. Instead of purely surveying cod, as NOAA has been, the study suggest that researchers take a more "ecosystem-based" approach. The study's leader believes that federal officials need to take into account temperature, climate forecasts, food availability, and reproductive rates, "to provide a more realistic picture of the potential size of fish stocks."

Now that it has become clear that previous models developed by NOAA government officials falsely represent the actual number of cod in New England, scientists and fisheries management must come together to

Of Whom Is Your Tree More Fond?

by

Victoria Lakes Freedman

Once upon a time, in a town much the same as yours, lived two sisters, Vendalia and Delonia.

Vendalia had the most beautiful blue eyes you could ever imagine. Her hair was dark brown, with just a hint of curl in it.

Delonia had nice eyes, too. They were not as big as Vendalia's eyes, and the blue was not quite as deep. But her hair had many lovely shades of blonde, all coming together to form beautiful golden curls.

Vendalia and Delonia loved each other very much, as well they should. They both loved their mother and each sister wanted Mother to love her the most. They were constantly competing with each other for Mother's love.

Now . . . If you are very quiet and pay close attention, you will hear all about a great adventure that these girls recently experienced.

THE AMAZING ANDREW'S GIGGLE VOCABULARY
Victoria L. Freedman - April 9, 2017

When I was born I decided not to talk until I was three . . . one-two-three years old. I couldn't count on my itty-bitty fingers yet, but boy oh boy did I have a lot going on in my mind.

Pretty much each day was much like the other for quite a while.
I ate!
I slept!
I messed my britches - that's what my Moie called my diapers.

Sometimes I was lonely and my Momma was busy trying to get much needed sleep. You see, I didn't come out of her the usual way - evidently she has a zipper on her belly and I pushed real hard and there she was. Wow! She was pretty!!! Blonde curly hair.

Well, this coming out caused her and me to be very tired. I slept all curled up, but then someone put water all over me. Why were they putting water all over me? I just came out of water!

Now those people finally stopped and I got to rest again. Whew! This being outside of the belly was a lot of work.

Evidently my Momma's belly zipper broke, so I heard them talking later that she got something called stitches and she didn't have to even have her belly opened up again unless she wanted another baby to come out off it.

With me as the AMAZING Andrew she probably wouldn't need another baby. I was, and still am, AMAZING. Plus, she really, really loves me.

She talks to me all the time and I talk to her with my smiling eyes and giggles. She loves my giggles.

She loves them so much that one day when I was in my swing - the one that goes side to side, not back and forth. Momma put a blanket over my teeny-weeny feet as the swing moved side to side all by itself. Some kind of magic I suppose.

27

Anyway, I wanted to communicate with Momma so I kicked the blanket off. She picked it up and put it back over my legs. I did this one-two-three-four times; still can't count on my little fingers. I'm only two months old.

On the fifth time I giggled the loudest giggle any Momma has ever heard. And I couldn't stop until finally Momma got tired of bending over and picking up the blanket. I guess all that giggling tired me out too, because it was in-the-swing nap time.

While nodding off I heard Momma talking to someone on the phone who she called "Momma". I reckon Momma's Momma is my Moie because the next day she came to our house. Momma put me in the swing even though Moie wanted to hold me a bit longer.

The swing moves side to side, the blanket goes over my feet and I KICK IT OFF. Moie puts it back over my feet. Momma says: Now just wait and see what he does next.

Moie quietly picked up the kicked-off blanket one-two-three-four-five more times, and on the sixth pick-up I giggle just a little bit.

My giggles were like words. Not all words have the same intensity. I know that I use big words.

When we get to know each other more as we become friends, I'll amaze you with even a bigger vocabulary - another big word. I'm full of them.

Momma started to giggle. So to show more my bigger words I giggle bigger and bigger. Momma was giggling so hard her face got a little red. Moie giggled, too. Then I gave out the great big giggle and Moie giggled so hard she had to sit down.

Oddly enough we didn't need naps this time, We just eye, smile giggled and word-talked to each other. Oh! I forgot. They also talked using their hands, something called sign language. I couldn't do that because my fingers were so itty-bitty, but boy, didn't I try!

We talked until Mom had to go and take my wonderful cousin Gabrielle to dance class.

Next time I'll tell you how I eventually talked in regular words. Bye!

I ♥ MY moie

The Grinch

by my Emmaler

30

"Charles"

su

Conde Nast
  Publication
    1 WORLD TRADE CENTER
  92nd FLOOR
N.Y. NY 10007

HELP! HELP!!

SYSTEM Help!

Your ... WITH ... your order ... on the back of your magazine ...

On hold

♫ Nice classical music.

Please take your time "I" will wait for you.

411 = The New Yorker Magazine

Please remain holding until the next representative

ALL

I

WANT

IS

Press 2 for payment

4/17/2017

Push 1 for Subscription Renewal

(800) 825-2510

The ___ **BLANK**

BLANKETY

"If I am not ever a subscriber"

Thank you for your patience

still holding

ADDRESS

Thank you Charles = Charles-In-IOWA-

Tori Lakes
FREEDOM ...

IF I WERE A DAVEY CAKES
by
The Godmoie

If I were a Davey Cakes,
what is it that I would be?
Could I pop into a bakery
and order a dozen of me?

Perhaps I'd be a cake of soap
with which to cleanse my body.
Or I could be a deodorized bar
which sure could help my Uncle Roddie.

I've been told, to be a Davey Cakes
is to be a thing of wonder.
A thing of joy forever
unless that statement is a blunder.

David is the name most called
to get my focused attention;
but Dave and David William
are also in contention.

But if a Davey Cakes is a joy forever,
does everyone agree?
Maybe not everyone,
but definitely The Godmother, definitely she.

Davey Cakes is a special name
given to me by a loved one.
I will wear and answer to it proudly,
for I am a special Godson.

After Accident
The Gulson

Shasha

1996

The characters:
BULLWINKLE The Moose
GEORGE Burns
GRACIE Allen
MARILYN Monroe
MRS SHAKESPEARE (wife of William)
****

GEORGE

Oh, Gracie.

GRACIE
Yes, George?

GEORGE

Would you say it's getting colder outside?

GRACIE

O.K., George . . . . You're a taxi!

GEORGE

Huh? What's that supposed to mean?

MRS SHAKESPEARE

I can never understand what my William is talking about, either. All those archaic cliches and that relentless compulsive rhyming!

GRACIE

Well, George, last week you asked me to call you a taxi. And I said, "O.K., George, you're a taxi!", and everybody laughed. Even the French people. I just thought we could use a little humor right now, so . . .

MARILYN

(Always breathy) So you decided to call him a taxi again?

~~GRACIE~~

GRACIE

Exactly !

GEORGE

I see. . . . Anyway, I'm getting ready to go for a walk and I was just wondering if you'd say it was getting coldàer outside.

GRACIE

O.K., George. (A little louder) It was getting colder outside. (Short pause)
(In normal tone) But that's still not as funny as the taxi thing, is it?

MRS SHAKESPEARE

My William never makes me laugh, either.

MARILYN

Is he a taxi, too?

GRACIE

I had an uncle once who was a taxidermist.

BULLWINKLE

I had a uncle twice who was in a taxi and in a dermatologist's office at the same time.

MARILYN

How could that happen?

BULLWINKLE

He was twins.

GRACIE

That's a pretty rocky joke, Bullwinkle.

BULLWINKLE

(Quizzically) Rocky?

MARILYN

MARILYN

I just love those movies!

GEORGE

What movies?

MARILYN

You know. The ones where Sylvester keeps getting beaten to a bloody pulp and everybody thinks he's some kind of hero for letting that happen to him.

GRACIE

I like the ones where Sylvester is always getting outsmarted by Tweety Bird.

MRS SHAKESPEARE

That's a different Sylviester, Gracie.

GRACIE

Yes, but it's the same cute little canary every time.

GEORGE

When you're right, you're right, Gracie.

BULLWINKLE

(Excitedly) The telephone is ringin'! The telephone is ringin'!

MARILYN

Wrong radio show, Bullwinkle!

BULLWINKLE

What radio show? The telephone is ringin'!

GRACIE

Oh, I'll get it. . . . Hello? Yes, she is. Well, goodbye now. What? Oooh, you want to talk to her? Hold the line please.

GEORGE

It must be a football player.

GRACIE

It's for you, Mrs Shakespeare.

MRS SHAKESPEARE

But I don't know any football players.

MARILYN

Oh, I do! Maybe it's for me.

MRS SHAKESPEARE

(On the phone) Yes? . . . Oh, it's you, William (Pause) What? You have a question for me?
(Pause) Well, I told you, I don't have any idea! . . . Look, be if you want to be, and don't be if
you don't want to. . . . O.K. You're welcome, William. Goodbye.
(Off the phone) For the past eleven evenings he's been bothering me with that same stupid
question.

GEORGE

That" would make this the twelfth night, then, wouldn't it?

MRS SHAKESPEARE

I suppose so. William is always making such an ado about nothing!

GEORGE

That thing's a play!

BULLWINKLE

No, the play's the thing.

MARILYN

No, The Thing is a movie. I remember I was so scared at the part when . . .

GEORGE

(Interrupting) Again with the movies.

BULLWINKLE

41

BULLWINKLE

I had an uncle once who was in the movies twice.

GRACIE

Yes, we know. He was twins.

BULLWINKLE

Nope. He went to the Palace Theatre and saw Gone With The Wind on Friday, and then he went to see Sister Carrie at the Bijou the next day.

MRS SHAKESPEARE

I didn't know you had a sister, Mr. Moose.

BULLWINKLE

Haven't you ever heard of a Caribou? Hee-hee! Get it?

GEORGE

We got it. We got it.

MARILYN

I got the flu once.

GRACIE

I had an uncle who flew once.

BULLWINKLE

And boy, were his arms tired?

GEORGE

Wouldn't yours be?

BULLWINKLE

No, I'd go in an airplane.

MARILYN

Airplane was such a funny movie!

MRS SHAKESPEARE

But a caribou isn't a moose. It's a reindeer.

BULLWINKLE

No, the sun's out, Honey.

MARILYN

I played the role of Honey when I was in Some Like It Hot.

GRACIE

I wouldn't mind a cinnamon roll right now.

BULLWINKLE

How about a drum roll?

GEORGE

We'd better drum up some laughs pretty soon or we'll all be in the market for a new job.

MRS SHAKESPEARE

I went to the Flea Market yesterday, but they were out of fleas.

GRACIE

Hey. That should have been my line!

MRS SHAKESPEARE

Then what's my line?

MARILYN

That was a television show.

BULLWINKLE

Not a movie, Blondie?

MARILYN

Sure, there were a lot of Blondie movies. Remember the one when Dagwood and little Alexander . . .

Robert Freedman - keyboards, arranger, musical director

Brian Moore - keyboards

Ted Perlman - guitar

Tranka (Tancredo de Oliveirea) - guitar

Gil Silva - guitar

Donald Moore - bass

Michael Tobas - drums

Daniel Diaz - percussion

Falumi Prince - percussion, vocalist

Sivuca (Severino Dias de Oliveirea) - guitar, accordian

Diva Gray

Sue Simmons

Arthur Williams

Melvin Edmondson

Larry Campbell

Victoria L. Freedman

9 Maple St., Salisbury, MA. 01950

Birth Date 4/27/48   Phone 465-1174

Tori Lakes Freedman
GOOD AT GETTING THINGS DONE
ACTOR • WRITER
Time Management/Observation/Stage Manager

ARTIST

P.O Box 1298 Scottsdale, AZ 85252
arranger99@cox.net
Phone: 480-539-3999 Cell: 480-799-7073

EDUCATION

1) High School graduate (1966)

2) 2 yrs. study leading to certification as Registered Radiological Technologist (graduated 1968)

3) Certified by American Red Cross for Standard First Aid and Personal Safety

PROFESSIONAL EXPERIENCE

1) X-ray Tech.
   a) Lake County Memorial Hospital, Willoughby, Ohio
   b) Lakeland Medical Bldg., Euclid, Ohio

2) Stage Manager/Asst. Director/Actress
   a) for several New York City theatrical productions
      (member of Actors' Equity Assc., professional
       name, Tori Lakes)

LIFE EXPERIENCE

1) Had major responsibility of raising six siblings

2) Traveled extensively in North American, Europe and Japan

PRIMARY INTRESTS

1) Warm blooded animals (gorillas in particular)
   a) I share my home with a beautiful rottweiller, a lovable
      basset hound and an inquisitive chow chow.

2) Animal rights   3) Photography

4) Babies   5) Crocheting

6) Watching the ocean   7) Ecology and Conservation

8) Reading   9) Visiting Zoos & Aquariums

10) Tape collection of old radio shows

GOALS

To further my education in order to interrelate with gorillas.

It's My Turn!
Torila: JRT's Shiksa
P.O Box 991
Scottsdale, AZ 85252

Hez the FEZ

~~Hez the FEX~~

A story by

Tori Lakes FREEDMAN

dedicated te Heather Diane
Baillargen = daughter

and

Gabrielle Adaire Baillargeon

granddaughter and at one
time in her life know
as little Mo
NOT TO BE CONFUSED with
little Hezzy

Thank you Brittany for the
use of your ~~the~~ table, we'll
always remember the
Capuchin Monkey NAMed Mango

April 15, 2017

46

April 15, 2017

Hez is a FEZ

Being a felt hat and red can be an interesting life.

There are times when I can not go NO where — I mean Anywhere.

Actually I can't move At All on my own. I require an accident by A cat or dog or people. Possibly a bird could help.

The wind is my best friend for movement It lets me move farther and faster than by A cat or a dog or people.

A cat can be annoying. They have these little pointy things on the end of their paws. They can hurt.

Don't get me wrong, the cat is not purposely trying to hurt me that's just the way they are built. It's fun when the cat toss me up in the air and the I fall to the floor. Sometimes I fall to the the couch or the table.

One time I fell to the top of the hot stove that was A SCARY situation. The Flames started to hurt my felt. That's what is great about a cat, they can jump up on things and that's exactly what happened. The cat got to the sink and pulled up that WATER SPRAYER.

so small I would cover them.
Wait, I know, I could sit on
a Shoebill Stork's head. That

Could be very interesting. Did
you know that Shoebill Storks
can stand real still for a
really long time. I mean a
really long time.

One day my friends Gabriella
Adaire and her Moie were at
the San Diego Park Zoo — a
wildlife place. I should go there
some day. Anyway there they
were mostly spending time
watching the GORILLAS. Moie
loves them, they changed her
life ever since she met C.C.,
a male silverback back in
July of 1976 AT THE Central
Park Zoo in Manhattan, that's
in New York City.

Well Gabadaire & her Moie
were taking a lunch break in
the shade, while sitting at the
out-door picnic table

And in no time I felt good
again. That's funny, did you
hear what I just said? I felt
good again.

I am a felt hat and I felt
good again. Thanks for laughing.

A dog likes to slobber on
everything. That means make
everything wet. They put every
THING in their mouths, you
know like human babies do.

They chew & chew & chew &
chew — they don't swallow, they
just like to chew.
I can't chew, I have no
mouth. What I can do is sit on
a person's head. Dogs & cats don't
like me sitting on their heads; they
just shake me off.
I suppose I could try to sit
on a birds, but many of them are

48

They were watching the wild life at a pond with an island in the middle. They were just chatting, they love each other very much, watching nature. There was this big bird, lovely bird with a huge bill but it was a statue. They thought it interesting to have a wildlife statue in amongst the wildlife.

They talked, watched and chewed. They have mouths! And guess what! Moie remarked about she thought she saw the statue move. Then Gabadaine thought maybe the statue moved. And then finally there was no doubt the statue was not a statue it was a real beautiful Shoebill stork.

I am definitely going to go to that zoo. I hope Gabadaine THE END

And here Moie will take me. They are people so they could put me in their suitcases. I can just rest in there.

Suitcases are easy for me because I don't breathe, eat or go to the bathroom. Suitcases can go in my types of vehicles. They can go in a car, a truck, a plane, a boat, a bike, then they have to be very small.

Hey! I am very small. I can even be tucked under an arm. The problem with that is sometimes Fez is getting accidentally dropped. Not to worry either a cat or a dog or a person will come along and I will be on the move again. And as always there is the wind.

I think it would be great to wait for a shoebill stork! Yes indeed.

DON'T CALL ME MAXI BABY
by
Victoria Lakes Freedman

My name is Maxwell.

Everyone in my family calls me Max.

Everyone in my family, that is, except my oldest sister.

She calls me Maxi Baby.

She will say, "Maxi Baby, come here."

I tell her my name is Max, not Maxi Baby.

Sometimes my sister bakes chocolate chip cookies.

I don't have to ask if I can help.

She always asks, "Maxi Baby, would you like to help me make cookies?"

I say, "Yes, but don't call me Maxi Baby."

I really like helping make chocolate chip cookies, but mostly I like eating them.

Sometimes my sister asks me to help fold the clothes that are still warm from the clothes dryer.

She'll say, "Maxi Baby, do you want to help fold clothes?"

I really do like to help, especially on cold days. Most of the time we fold clothes while watching cartoons on television.

Still, I don't like to be called Maxi Baby.

Lots of times, when everyone in the family is busy, I ask my sister to play with me.

Often she will stop what she is doing and say, "O.K., Maxi Baby, what do you want to play?"

Then I say I want to play a game; and I also tell her that my name is Max, not maxi Baby.

Once in a while my sister will say, "Hey, Maxi baby, how would you like to go to our special restaurant for lunch?"

Naturally I say I want to go, but then I say, angrily, "Don't call me Maxi Baby!"

A couple of days ago, without my asking, my sister offered to read me my favorite story.

She Said, "Maxi baby, if you come and sit by me I'll read to you about Mister Rabbit."

I got very angry and yelled, "I am not a baby!"

She said she knew I wasn't a baby. So I asked her why she always calls me Maxi baby.

"It's a word of endearment," she said. "Some people say honey, sweetheart, or maybe lovey-dovey, darling, or sweetie-pie, and so forth. I call you Maxi Baby. It's just my way of telling you that I love you."

Boy, did I ever feel like a creep!

Here I had been yelling at her all this time because I thought she was calling me a baby.

What can a guy do?! I mean, she is very nice to me. She seems to love me a lot.

O.K., so what can it hurt? I'll let her call me Maxi Baby.

Still, to everyone else my name is Max.

DON'T CALL ME MAXI BABY!

THE END

Heather the Feather Goes to School

by
Victoria Lakes Freedman

Heather is a feather that flies through the air. She can go almost anywhere.

One day she floated into a classroom filled with girls and boys.

"Children," said the teacher, "it is time for your math lesson, so put away the toys."

The toys put away, the math lesson begins. The boys and girls count by fives and by tens.

"Fifty is the number of states, at present, Miss Pomtree."

"That is correct, Joseph," replied Miss Pomtree. "Now, Mark, what is the capital of these United States?"

"The capital is Washington, D.C.," Mark replied without haste.

Class, if you would want to see the Mississippi River at its mouth, in which direction would you travel from Arkansas, east, west, north or south?"

Before anyone could answer Miss Pomtree's last question, a bell rang to indicate the end of this geography session; but do you know the answer to that last question?

The students were eager to be dismissed from school, but they had to wait for permission from the teacher, that is the rule.

This school day has ended and only Heather the Feather is left behind. Soon a breeze will come and carry her off to a new adventure . . .
. . . so she doesn't mind.

The End

BERNIE'S DINER & DELI

Bob Freedman, ASCAP, & Tori Lakes Freedman

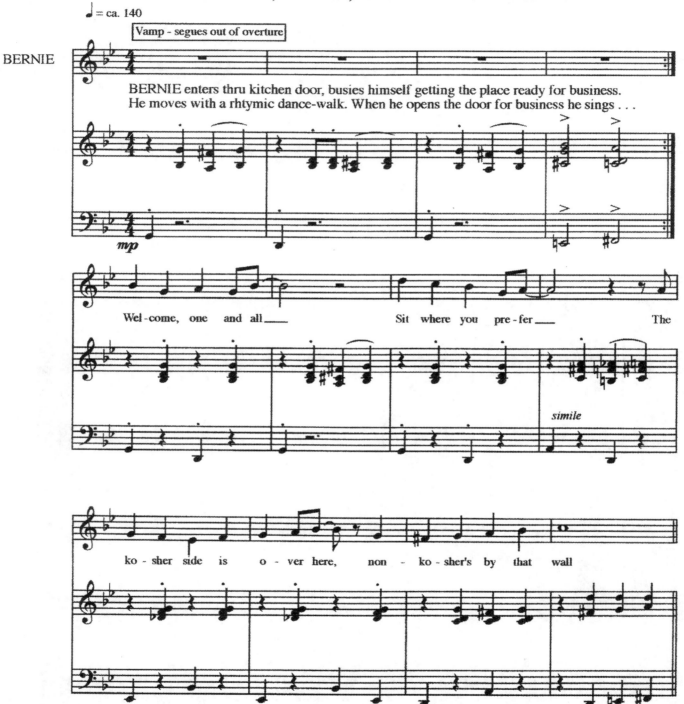

BERNIE enters thru kitchen door, busies himself getting the place ready for business.
He moves with a rhtymic dance-walk. When he opens the door for business he sings . . .

Wel-come, one and all___ Sit where you pre-fer___ The

ko-sher side is o-ver here, non-ko-sher's by that wall

Have a steak, a bowl of soup, Our pies will throw you for a loop.

Interlude

Bernie schmoozes with the customers

Peo - ple meet peo - ple here May - be they make friends

THE GUY WHO THOUGHT HE WAS THE BOSS

by Tori Lakes Freedman

He is the head =patriarc of acting brothers
He is the father of two.

He is a man of many gifts and he will be happy
to name more than a few.

He is tall, He is dark, he is sweet & sometimes sad.

Yet all who know him love him, but boy can he be bad.

If I got a chance to work him, he could
learn a lot from me.

He'll think he can't because he is truely talented.
Yet I can teach him how to truely be.

Not the hamlet to be, but the
Dudes to be.

I'll educate him on the ways of the Dudes
and he will cry Whoopee!!

THE END

April 16, 2017

The Next
art wor is by the

she makes → happy →

Happy tap

Happy

India Rose

as well as her Momma and

her Daddy + grand parents

great grand parents

* Harper has Scottish accent. Shr11 gets the Shermans some

We three met at Office Max on Hayden and Osborn — Sept. 8, 2019 due to Office Maxes continued

Jessicaeres = Marvelous. *

and the 60 is even better of it.

Didn't get it right Office Max on Stapley

at India Rose is an art student
at A. S. U.

As Always it takes All of
US Dude Sq̶u̶ Squad

Alumeni → to help all past,
present and future Dude Squad
Dude.

Our main Dude is the best
Friend Anyone could ever have:

He & K̶e̶l̶l̶y̶
are happy   DAVID   FAR
Makers   OUT

LEE DAY   June 1966
            JAN 2017

Findlay Ohio & little Tommy Day is Cool!

A Rose
By any
NAME
other
WOULD
Be

C
A
L
L
E
D

India Rose

Indiarosechudnow@gmail.com

Tori Lakes Freedman

It's My Turn!
Torila: JRT's Shiksa
P.O Box 991
Scottsdale. AZ 85252

Wife of Bob Freedman , Momma to Heather Diane and Kellie Sharon (Ward), Moie to Gabrielle Adaire, Emmalee Vendalia and Willoughbie Hannah Light. Step mother, well actually Tori to Robert Seth Freedman and Mellisa Jane Freedman. Granny T to Rory Robson Baker, Jordan David Peterson, Amy Nicole and Steven Alexander Mc Clellan. The godmother to David William Appleby and Hollie Jean Kooyman. The godmoie to Jordan Davis Kooyman and Sahsa E. Appleby. The best friend to Marj Davis Appleby and Diane Ellen Harris Bohana.

I am the eldest :Sissey of David Sherman Lakes Messer (long story), Rockey Walter Kummer, Rickey Earl Kummer. Kummer was originally spelled Coomer but for some reason Sailor decided to change it. Randey Jack Kummer, Tamela (Tammalyn) Kummer Bartlett, and the last Kummer is Troy Melvin (Troy Boy) Now for the Youngs : David, Douglas (Dougy Pooh, and Rhonda Kay Green. Robert Maxwell Lakes and Kathryn Victoria (Thrynie) Lakes. Plus at Least three more a boy named Mike and two girls. Those three were the only ones I did nor help raise. George Ann Lakes is my stepmother (she's only five years older than I). My mother thought her real name was Virginia Lee Messer. In fact her real birth certificate reads Margaret Virginia Dunn.

Back to NYC! Studied voice with David Ralph at the Astoria. The only furniture was in his apartment was a beautiful black baby grand with bench and in the far left corner was a mattress on the floor. Wonderful supportive coach, but wouldn't let me sing my husband's song, "Beautiful Music", because because it was too difficult for my really beginning vocal skill. Instead he chose from My Fair Lady, SHOW ME; and boy did I show him. Took tap with, I'm ashamed to admit that I have temporarily misplaced his name but when I finally unpack our albums I will rectify that. The dance Studio was over the Little Carnegie Theater. Every class ended with the same routine. Pah dah, pah dah, pah dah pah. Pah dah, pah dah, pah dah pah. Pah dah ball change, pah dah ball. Flap, flap, flalp, bawm bawm! He would also say to me at the end of class, your too good for the beginners class, but

68

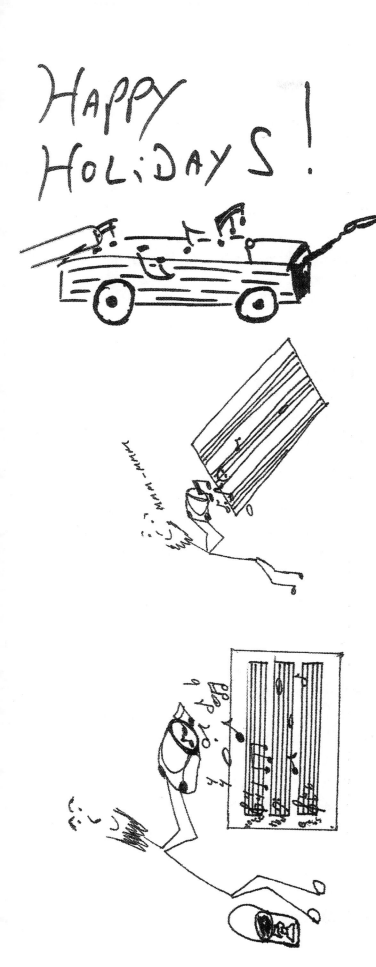

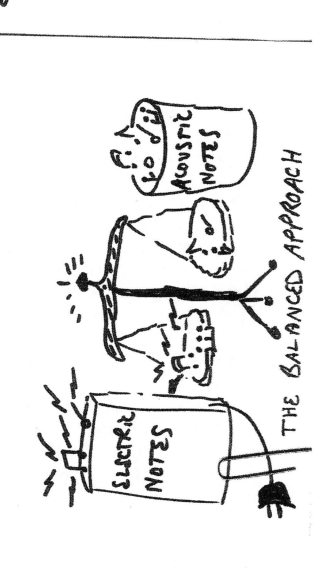

at least move front so that real beginners can learn from you. Somebody out there must know him from this routine.

Out of H B studios grew the Inner Circle Ensemble. We put on a production of Come Blow Your Horn. Frank Sariccino payed the lead. He looked very much like James Dean. There is a friend of mine who works at the Cotsco and his real name is James Dean; he goes by J.D.. I have a nephew who's name is Jack David and he goes by J.D..

Before Come Blow Your Horn, our first (and for free) in front of an audience was in someone's friend's dance loft. We did the "Well" scene. I couldn't hear my cue and since I hadn't become a stage manager yet I couldn't get me out there...my fellow ICE members didn't alert me so the beginning of the "Well" scene went on much longer than probably ever before. The two ICE actors, yes that's when all male and female, thespian's became ACTORS, sitting on the couch never broke character. BravOoovAaa!

Then we did "A Sign in Sydney Brustein's Window" at a large space owned owned by George and during rehearsal Paul Sorvino joined his friend to see the space. It was on 10th and not far from Studio 54. It had been decided by all ICE members that I was deemed most responsible so therefore, I was the "walking till". I bet Walt Whitcover had something to do with that 'cause he knew us all. I was never asked, just given the money after our first show.

Bo Walker was one of the few of us (and Michael Perieser) who actually had real show business jobs, had a dilemma. His Mom was coming to town and he had a gig at the White Barn Theater in Westport, Conn. So he took me to see the director, Marc Gordon, and producer and I got my first Stage manager job. The play was "An Act of Kindness'----real upbeat drama. My sister who was 15 at the time was staying with us. The director begrudgingly drove us up but did not tell us he wasn't driving us back. We slept in bunk beds under the stage. We had a good time.

Now I'm not sure how I found myself as an ASM to the SM Lynn Gutter at JRT for "Benya the King" (probably Bo), BUT THERE I WAS. My first duty was to mop the floor of the very small flat concrete floor. I did it well, had a lot of practice. Then I got to put the fake blood in the tin that was nailed to the upright piano 'cause somebody was going to get shot. That was filled with blanks by me (boy, trusted with the company's money, now with a gun) and was the first and last time I have ever touched a gun.

I reckon Lynn wanted to go back to writing because Ran Avni called me to meet with him and the director Lynn Polan (her sister's name is Mary-Lake and handsome boyfriend name is Tom. That was our production of "Greenfields". Very interesting group of people. The Rebbe was played by Marc Nelson, he has been on CHUNG! CHUNG!=LAW AND ORDER at least twice. Steve Horowitz, who also appeared on Law And Order, was the second actor to play Melvin. Laralu Smith, ? Gusty played the girls. The young man who's name I have forgotten but I will never forget how he could sit on his haunches and his legs repeatedly. I could have watched that ability of his for the whole first act and but I had a show to run and he had other business do on stage. I think it was that multi-talented sweet and generous actor's uncle who let us borrow his balalaika —spell check did not agree with my spelling of this guitar style beautiful instrument. As I was saying before spell check so rudely interrupted, now that was a trustful uncle. Maybe he was not aware of the ways of poor show folk.

The first lovely and warm LADY who played the mother got in an auto accident and was then replaced by Harry Belafonte's (what say Belafonte?) acting coach. I learned that by seeing Harry in the audience before the show while looking out of Jewish school kitchen window into the stage=audience space. I went out and asked Harry what was he doing here. I didn't figure that he came to see my magnificent skills as a stage manager because he just knew me as Tori, wife (and little lady he liked to pick up in his arms) to Bob, his musical director.
There's another Harry tie in. The good non professional actor, Alan Brandt, who played the father, hosted the wrap up party at his HUGE apartment on West End Avenue. He had a lot of African tribal masks on the walls and I mentioned that I had a friend who also collected them. I told him, Harry Belafonte. OH————no it was more like an—oh yes. He smiled his wife called to him and he politely excused himself and walked through the crowd. Take that Harry.

Thank you for blessing us and being my angel.
With LOVE & THANKS,

Andrew and The Burkhart Family

Lori, 2019
Sept. 15,
3:15 A.M.

IF I WERE A DAVEY CAKES
by
The Godmoie

If I were a Davey Cakes,
what is it that I would be?
Could I pop into a bakery
and order a dozen of me?

Perhaps I'd be a cake of soap
with which to cleanse my body.
Or I could be a deodorized bar
which sure could help my Uncle Roddie.

I've been told, to be a Davey Cakes
is to be a thing of wonder.
A thing of joy forever
unless that statement is a blunder.

David is the name most called
to get my focused attention;
but Dave and David William
are also in contention.

But if a Davey Cakes is a joy forever,
does everyone agree?
Maybe not everyone,
but definitely The Godmother, definitely she.

Davey Cakes is a special name
given to me by a loved one.
I will wear and answer to it proudly,
for I am a special Godson.

?? R.! ↓

↑ ↑ Smiles

↑ Views me through Kellie Ward Burkhart's eyes.

Scorpio Audio Technologies
24400 Highland Rd * # 88 * Richmond Hts OH 44143
216/486-8046 FAX 216/486-9758
Email: scorpio@scorpioaudio.com

FAX TRANSMITTAL

COMPANY:

TO: THE GODMOTHER   **FAX: 1-480-926-9157**

FROM: David (the Godson) and Marj (your forever friend)

DATE: 07/11/00   **PAGES (including cover sheet):____ 1 ____**

Hello Godmother,

Thank you for the thoughtful gifts. Just in time, my old wallet is about to give up. The frame will go nicely in our new house! Yes, I said " our new house". Marianne and I have purchased a home in South Euclid. It is a nice brick bungalow and is about a 6.5-minute drive from the studio. I will send some pictures when we get it cleaned up.

I hope every thing is going well.
Thanks again, David

GREETINGS! I'm trying to come your way in January, a few days in front of a Designer's Conference in the Tucson area, then a few days with an old classmate in Sonita! Keep your fingers crossed. Hope all is well there and that all the babies are wonderful…Since there will be a few others traveling with me, we'll stay at a Marriott close to you. Which one would be better? We'll get from the airport to the hotel and just park it there until we rent a car to drive to Tucson for the conference. Let me know!!!
Love to one and all…. Marj

BABY SASHA
by
THE GODMOIE

Did you hear a bell ring today?

SASHA! SASHA!, SASHA! SASHA!

Was there a sweet smelling breeze this day?

SASHA! SASHA!, SASHA! SASHA!

Have you felt a moment of pure joy today?

SASHA! SASHA!, SASHA! SASHA!

Were there bright colored flowers this day?

SASHA! SASHA!, SASHA! SASHA!

Can you remember something special today?

SASHA! SASHA!, SASHA! SASHA!

Twas it lovely to be with family this day?

SASHA! SASHA!, SASHA! SASHA!

Were there giggles today?

SASHA! SASHA!, SASHA! SASHA!

To hear, smell, feel, see, be, enjoy happiness in all its forms this day and every day to your Mommy and Daddy MEANS.........

SASHA! SASHA! SASHA! SASHA! SASHA!

The Valley of the Sun.

Randy is a great guy—doesn't want company bigger—he's comfortable with that.

makes you want to go ____ While I'm

cruis - in' in my chec - ro - let

spoken: 'Til I see ye next time, André!

THANK YOU 1976
THANK YOU
THANK YOU
THANK YOU
THANK YOU
THANK YOU
THANK YOU
THANK YOU
THANK YOU
THANK YOU
THANK YOU
THANK YOU
THANK YOU
THANK YOU
THANK YOU
THANK YOU
THANK YOU
THANK YOU

THANK YOU
1997

Lullaby For All My Babies

Words & music by Tori Lakes Freedman

Piano accompaniment by
Bob Freedman

Lullaby for All My Babies

In June* of 2017 I took
My statue of Gorilla & Baby to the
Scottsdale Osborn Hospital to cheer
up Rowbear. I did not expect that
Rowbear and Kellie and Andrew Lincoln and
Heather and Michael and Gabrielle and
Emmalee and Finally Willoughbie were
                going to send me on an unexpected
*It have been   long layover, at Blythe and
a bit earlier   Palm Springs, California.

The Things You Can Get Done At Costco
Tori Lakes Freedman

that's where I started this

Blue Moon over Kentucky Bill, did give us
The song will have no dyin' Momma
The song will have no boozin' redneck
The song will have no pickup trucks

No hangin' out in honky-tonks
If your kids can't go there
WE WON'T GO THERE
We're just about havin' clean ol' fun

Dancin' is HAPPY, Singin' is HAPPY
We'll tap our foot
We'll kick our heels
We'll reel all around the clock

Put on your tap shoes
Cover up your midriffs
Put that SMILE FIRMLY ON
Over here! Square dancin' has just begun

Bring your Irish drum
Get your Irish bagpipes
Bring your Irish "y'all"
and your Irish or Scottish tea

Do-si-do, do-si-dee, do-si-thee
Color if you want to
But don't stay in the lines
Bright oranges and green will be fine

Color is what the world is
Without the ugly gray
Gray is what gunfire is
The gray is smelly, too

The gray attracts the Haters
haters like Dumb and Dumber
Are on the tube twenty-four hours a day
The haters won the vote, unfortunately

We will have only one truck
The dump truck it will be
We'll escort the Haters to the bucket
Not the one with the hole in it, dear Liza, dear Liza

Janet thank you for the word of
The thingy=hickydoo on the front
Of a truck by the name of Trump
Excuse me, what I meant to say was Dump

Do-si-do, grab your partner
Put on your ballet slippers
And prance across the floor
Grab clogs and your fancy togs

Allemande left, Allemande right
Play the Irish pipe and drum
We'll reel all day and all night
'All', we all are havin' is fun

Play the Irish drum
Or a snare drum will do
We'll thank ol' Bill for Bluegrass
Not in four time, but fast time

Play the viola, play the 'cello
We need at least one horn
A trumpet or a sassy sax or trombone
Oh! I got it, the penny whistle

Let Blake Shelton play the mandolin
Alison Krauss on the viola

Teddy "Steve" Perlman can play whatever he wants
And of course Bob Freedman will conduct

Now we got our band
We got our togs and shoes
Allemande, chassé, spin, jump
Some of us can do

Grab your partner gently
Boy or girl will do
Grab your instruments gently
Yeah, Blake, Alison and Steve, that means you

We're tuckered out from so much fun
We'll sing the "Lullaby For All My Babies"
Take your shoes off and rub your feet
It's time to say adieu

"Go to sleep my little one.
Tori's here with you
Dreamland is a wondrous place
I am very fond of you

"Dream of cotton candy clouds
High up in the sky
Dream of funny-faced clowns
I am very fond of you"

SHUUSH NOW! Night night

The End
and Finished

EMMALEELA
by
Tori Lakes Freedman

EMMALEELA is strong
EMMALEELA is bright
She moves about all the time
Which for her is not wrong

'Her smile' is what her Moie calls her
All around her must agree
She brings people together
Without her no one would want to be

She fought for Bernie and Hillary in 2016
Remember, that was the year when the FIRST lady won the numbers
The United States of America felt good about what they had done
But the Republicans and Russians made it otherwise
Now the President of the FREE world heads Dumb and Dumber

When history tells the story about
The bigots and chauvinists that took first place
Let it also declare how Trump and his gang were puppets all the while
Let it also declare how they went to the elite lockdown white collar space

When sanity returns to our country, and it must
Remember all who voted for Hillary knew she was the most prepared
She, like Emmaleela, will be there for us, in fact they are there now
Let there never be the the disaster of this time, which may make the free
world bust

When sanity returns to our country it will begin to heal
When sanity returns to our country may it please be now
When sanity returns to our country we will hold our heads up high
When sanity returns to our country again, as it must, let's keep repeating

Again I say, Remember the day of infamy
Don't let this break you down to where you no longer vote

d dinosaur
i ice cream
s saw
n nut
e eggs
y yak
l lion
a apple
n number
d dog

POEMS

AND

OTHERS

by
Tori Lakes Freedman

Tori Lakes Freedman
GOOD AT GETTING THINGS DONE

Time Management/Observation/Stage
Manager

P.O. Box 2269   Gilbert, AZ 85299

arranger99@cox.net

Phone 480-539-3999   Cell 480-799-7073

Rowbear Music
BOB FREEDMAN
Composer/Arranger

P.O. Box 2269
Gilbert, AZ 85299
Phone: (480) 539-3999
Email:
bfreedmanarranger@hotmail.com

THE LION AND THE FROG
BY: EMMALEE BAILLARGEON

ONE DAY A LION ATE A FROG.
HE HAD SHARP TEETH!
THE FROG WAS CRYING.
HE WAS SO SCARED!
THE FROG LICKED THE LION WITH HIS
TONGUE!
SPUTTOOIE HE SAID. THAT WAS GROSS.
THEN HE WENT TO FRY'S.
HE GOT FRIES AT FRY'S.
WE'LL MEET AGAIN FROG, SAID LION.

Little
Hezzie
↓↙
Sugardrop

Sugarplum

Sugarpot
↗↑
'Little'
Mo

Heath
e
r

Kellie

Sharon

WE ARE THE LADIES

Lyrics: Tori Lakes Freedman

Music: Robert M. Freedman, ASCAP

Teenage boy "Boss" says: Get working, girls! Not talking!
Server "Molly" says: He's a kid - and he calls US girls!

We Are The Ladies

We are la-dies, we are girls, we are wo-men, WE ARE LA-DIES!

16

Here we go a-gain. Peo-ple are hun-gry. They need to eat   They are hap-py and they are bu-sy, they

need us to help them   They are in a hur-ry!   They   will show   their

We are la-dies, we are girls,   we are wo-men, WE   ARE

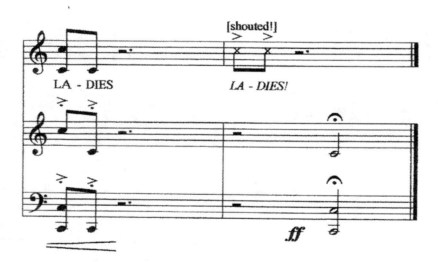

[shouted!]

LA - DIES   LA - DIES!

1st out of my body
Moi
2ND out of my body

Hez

Sugardrop

Sugarpot

Andrea
→

Your Moie loves ya A whole Mess! Baby boy :

The only too young to hug me without School Brush from his adults.

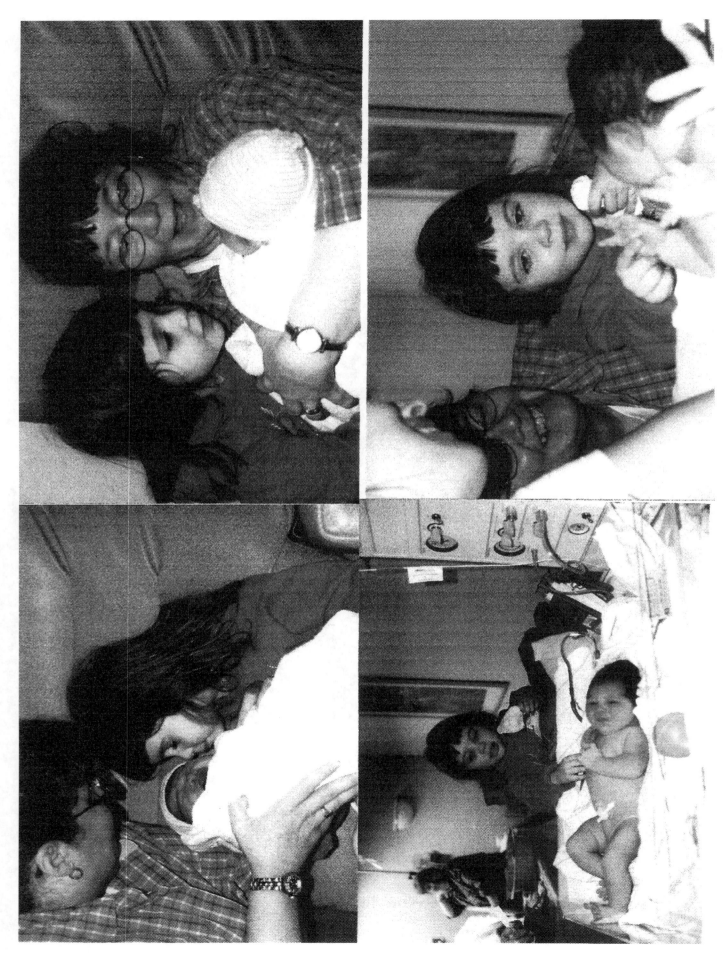

Song for Kellie

Robert M. Freedman, ASCAP

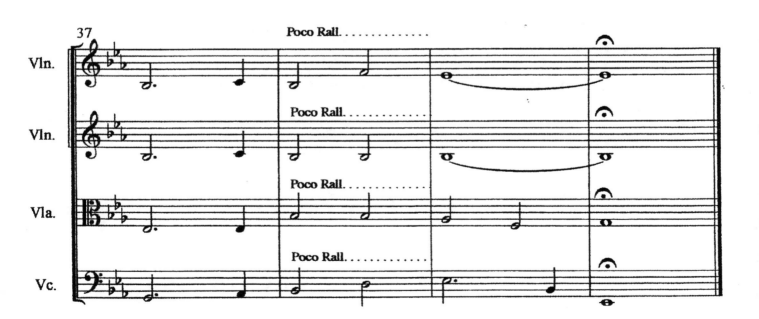

TOOTS -

YOUR DNA RESULTS CAME FROM
www.myheritagedna.com

IT SAYS YOU ARE

54.1% British and Irish

38.7 % Scandinavian

5.5% East European   ←the JRT's Shiska
                        Shiksa
0.9% Ashkenazi Jewish←   silly
                            Moi
0.8% Papuan

Online (not printable) it also lists a couple of hundred 4th cousins twice removed, etc.

→ ALSO, you are apparently subscribed to pay $14.00 a month - I'm not sure what for.

I will do what I can to unsubscribe you.

SEE ATTACHED PAGE ⟶

Where is

This is
Not Monday July 29, 2019
it is SUNDAY
28th of July

Tori Lakes Freedman
GOOD AT GETTING THINGS DONE
Time Management/Observation/Stage
Manager

P.O. Box 2269   Gilbert, AZ 85299
arranger99@cox.net

Phone 480-539-3999   Cell 480-799-7073

↗ that's from 2017

Patty Cake a young female gorilla that lived at the central park zoo with an Aunt Female gorilla Caroline or ~~Carolyn~~ Carolyn. They stayed together in the same compartment and had access to the outside through a door in the wall. Also there was a beautiful silverback who I call Cee Cee — don't know his given name.

Cee   NOBODY   Patty Cake
                              and Aunt

Cee-cee is responsible to All my things animal.

He is responsible for letting me know that I AM an animal person. Family dogs tried to tell me by sleeping with and Tiny, ~~little~~ chi would curl up in the bend of my legs/knees MA's while lying on my side. I never lived with Tiny. But she traveled with MA. At Mommy's house in Mentor.

111

Ohio lived Rocky, a GREAT DANE. So there is big-o-Rock, being out ~~witted~~ witted by little-itty-bitty TINY. TINY would go under Rocky, while he was ~~he was~~ standing and just stand under him, Didn't touch Rocky didn't Nip him, didn't GRAWL OR bark — ~~⊗~~ JUST STOOD THERE (not my brother Rockey — the dog came with the name) Poor pouch of the large VARIETY got all upset. ~~Can't laugh at that~~ ~~help~~ ~~but~~ CAN'T help but laugh at that sight, which I still see in my minds' eye.

Back to gorillas. Kent is a very special place. This rich guy started having different types of ANIMALS on his VAST estate. His son played with the young gorillas, in what could be called — A DRIVEWAY. By the time I learned about this guy + the various ~~free~~ ROAMING dear + the like, he had been getting more animals. He went into the gorillas enclosure. He played with the gorillas. They lived in family units gender, size, age all intermingled, there is footage ~~⊗~~ of this. One male gorilla enjoyed pulling out the eyelashes of the HUMAN MAN + would consume them. He pulled them out with his mouth. The big enclosure was the ~~first~~ of it's kind.

plus other connecting enclosures and hallways.

112

The House of Representatives
State of Hawaii

hereby presents this certificate to

THE GORILLA FOUNDATION

WHEREAS, mankind is merely a tenant on this unique and wondrously beautiful planet which we call Earth, our only home in the vastness of the universe, it is our responsibility to ensure that the fragile and delicate balance of the entire ecosystem is maintained; and

WHEREAS, the Legislature of the State of Hawaii is proud to recognize those organizations and individuals who are dedicated to the preservation and protection of endangered species, and who seek to improve the environmental conditions of wildlife habitats, as the people of Hawaii appreciate the beauty of nature, and understand that Hawaii, as one of the world's most geographically isolated landmasses, supports numerous plant, insect, and animal species found nowhere else on Earth; and

WHEREAS, THE GORILLA FOUNDATION, an internationally recognized and respected organization, with more than 45,000 members worldwide, has heightened the awareness of human relationships with animals and has sought to address the problems of endangered species worldwide; and

WHEREAS, Koko and Michael, the world renowned lowland gorillas, have been involved in the world's longest uninterrupted ape-language study project, using American Sign Language to communicate at THE GORILLA FOUNDATION; and

WHEREAS, THE GORILLA FOUNDATION has decided to relocate its important research projects to Maui, to provide a more natural environment for the gorillas, thus enhancing the gorilla's social adjustment, which will improve the quality of the research conducted there; now, therefore,

BE IT RESOLVED by the House of Representatives of the State of Hawaii of the Seventeenth Legislature, Regular Session of 1993, that this body hereby recognize and commends THE GORILLA FOUNDATION for protecting and preserving endangered species and welcomes them as new residents of Hawaii.

The _17th_ Legislature

Speaker of the House

Chief Clerk

Sponsoring Representative

114

ENTRY FORM FOR "PICTURE THIS" MONTHLY CONTEST

(PLEASE PRINT CLEARLY)

NAME _Tori Freedman_

Mailing ADDRESS _P. O. Box 87_

CITY _Woodburn_ STATE _KY_ ZIP _42170_

PHONE _(502) 781-5602_ DATE OF ENTRY _____

SUBJECT OF PICTURE _Gorilla Gorilla_

To Victoria,
Movements for real and lasting change are sustained by the
relationships we build with one another.
Thank you for your support.

Michelle Obama

Ellen of Degeneres

by

Tori Lakes Freedman

APRIL 17, 2017

She is petite. She is blonde.
She is sweet and she likes guests.
Her shows are how we know her and that is
fine and good, for she often know what's best.

Her hair is often short in length,
'cause she doesn't want to fuss.
But all have seen it much longer
and like it just as if she made that fuss.

People of all ages watch her show.
In fact I know a few.
Gabrielle, Emmalee, Willoughbie Hannah Light,
Heather Diane, wow that is more than two

One day she will have them on her show.
It is then they will share their interests.
These three plus one ladies have special skills and knowledge.
And each will say me first.

Gabrielle will teach her about sharks,
for few know more than she.
Emmalee will teach her how to be Cinderella 'cause
when she was two, that is all she wanted to be.

Willoughbie Hannah Light will teach her how to be
little Hezzy for she is certainly that.
Big Hezzy is Heather and she will teach her how to
be a mother to A wonderful threesome, not one a brat

119

THE More is from where they all sprang.
She will teach her that life is made for fun,
learning and to be true blue.
Most all who know her will happily tell her
that, that is certainly true.

That is why the world needs lots of love
and that is more than some.
Lots of love creates confidence.
Confidence breeds the threesome.

Ellen of Degeneres loves her mother, as well.
THERE is a lady who can teach us all how to see
the world in a half-full way.
Instead of that half-empty way
and be forthright will her tell!

Be happy all who watch her show
and don't envy her, her money.
For it is not easy to do what Ellen does
and that is to always be funny.

THE END

KELLIE

by
Victoria Lakes Freedman

Hello, my name is Kellie. What is your name?

That is a nice name.

My eyes are blue. Are your eyes blue, too?

Or are they green?

Or gray?

Or brown?

My dog has brown eyes. Do you have a dog? My dog is named Russell.

I play ball with my dog. We play in my back yard.

I throw the ball and my dog catches it in his mouth.

Sometimes my dog knocks me down. He does not knock me down on purpose. He is a big dog and I am a little girl.

Russell is my only pet.

My aunt has a rabbit for a pet.

My grandma has a parakeet with green and white feathers.

My uncle has lots of fish in a glass box. The box is called an aquarium. That is a hard word for me to say.

Can you say aquarium?

I wish we could talk all day. I like being with you but now it is time for me to feed Russell.

I hope you will visit me again. Good-bye. Have a happy day.

THE END

Preschool Fun! August & September

TORI'S RADIO PLAY - XMAS 2001
CAST OF CHARACTERS   *by Tori Lakes Freedman*

ANNOUNCER

SPADIAMOND

NEW YORK BAR LADY

CLAMMY HANDS GUY

THE LEVY TWINS (Girls: one sounds like a Bostonian and the other sounds like an Atlantan. They speak in unison or every other word or however the actors decide.)

EXTRAS (Whoever's not busy at the time)

FOLEY:
      foot steps and cheerful whistling
      sounds of claw pulling from skirt
      sounds of Clammy Hands Man getting up from the pavement
      street noise over the good-byes
      sounds of Clammy Hands Man walking away
      running footsteps
      screeching of stopping taxi
      aridfication
      traffic sounds
      sounds of dishes and silverware being placed on table

MUSIC:
      Theme music
      songs and singing drifting from the bars
      juke box music in soda shop

****

!
',"TORI'S RADIO PLAY - XMAS 2001

ANNOUNCER

Good day ladies and gentlemen and welcome to the first installment of soon to be your favorite private detective, Samuel Richard Spadiamond, brought to you by Blue Coal. There's a good warm feeling from the glow of Blue Coal as well as the satisfaction of knowing that it helps to create the refreshing acid rain that exfoliates the deciduous and evergreen trees down wind of your home town.^ So tonight at bath time crank up that heat and feel good that you are keeping your neighbors down wind of you from having to rake up those pesky autumn leaves. Blue Coal is the neighborly heating product, use it in good health. (cough,cough, cough)

Music

(THEME MUSIC FOR SHOW)

ANNOUNCER

AND NOW WITH NO FURTHER DELAY BLUE COAL BRINGS TO YOU, SAMUEL RICHARD SPADIAMOND, P.I.

FOLEY

(foot steps and cheerful whistling)

SPADIAMOND

It's quite relaxing to walk the streets of Filmnoirville in the late evening with the flickering of the neon lights and the smell of booze oozing from the beer joints, stepping over the odd tipsilated ejected bar patron, tipping one's fedora at the loveÙly leggy ladies....

NEW YORK BAR LADY

HEY! Mister, what do you think you're doin'? Keep your clammy hands to yourself.

CLAMMY HANDS GUY

Sorry, kid, seems my claw is caught on your nicely fitting straight skirt hem.
If you could just stand still I can try to detangle the SITuation.

NEW YORK LADY

Say! You pulling my leg or what?

CLAMMY HANDS GUY

Nah! Just trying to keep your threads intact.

SPADIAMOND

Hello there pretty lady, What are you and Clammy up to? Didn't know that you two where acquainted.

NY LADY

We ain't acquainted, we're attached.

SPADIAMOND

When's the big day?

NY LADY

What?

CLAMMY HANDS GUY

Hey, kid, hold still. Nothing is going to disattach unless you quit your squirming. Know what I mean?

FOLEY

(Traffic noises)

MUSIC

(songs and singing drifting from the bars)

EXTRAS

(mumblings of conversation of passers-by)

SPADIAMOND

Where's the honeymoon going to be?

NY LADY

Sammy Dick, are you drunk? I can't make any sense of what you are saying and why don't you get this guy off of me...

CLAMMY HANDS GUY

Look kid, if you don't do the cooperation thing your skirt is a gonner! And not only that....

NY LADY

Let go of my skirt, mister, or I'll have my USED to be friend here wallop you up along side of your head and if.....

Clammy HANDS GUY

P.I. man, is that you up there?

SPADIAMOND

How's things Clammy?

CLAMMY HANDS GUY

Could be worse, the caterpillar turned into a butterfly last week and flew the coop.

NY LADY

IF YOU TWO ARE FINISHED CATCHING UP ON THE DAY'S NEWS!!!!

SPADIAMOND and CLAMMY HANDS GUY

(in unison) Unh? What?

CLAMMY HANDS GUY

P.I. man, give me a hand here. I'm all tangled up in this kid's skirt.

SPADIAMOND

GOTCHA! Hey, pretty lady, Clammy here is stuck to your skirt and he needs you to hold still.
Here let me hold on to you until....

FOLEY

(sounds of claw pulling from skirt)

NY LADY

Oh, Sammy Dick. What a relief, I thought this guy was trying to get fresh.

SPADIAMOND

Pretty Lady, I'd like to introduce to you CLAMMY, a gentleman of integrity and good will, not to
mention a man of unusual handage.

FOLEY

(sounds of Clammy getting up from the pavement)

NY LADY

OOOhhh! Mr. Clammy, can you forgive my rudeness of misunderstanding?

CLAMMY HANDS GUY

No problem kid, already forgotten. Say P.I. man, you joining the crowd at Murphy O'Shea's next
week?

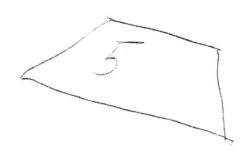

SPADIAMOND

Wouldn't miss it, Clammy my man, wouldn't miss it.

FOLEY

(street noise over the good-byes)

CLAMMY HANDS MAN

Catch you later P.I.man.   Unusual meeting you, kid.

FOLEY

(sounds of Clammy walking away)

EXTRAS

(street crowd mumblings)

SPADIAMOND

It's too noisy out here; let's pop into Franky's for a tall cool one.

NY LADY

No can do, Sammy Dick, I'm on my way to choir practice.

SPADIAMOND

Didn't know you were a church regular.

NY LADY

I'm not. I am a choir practice regular; it's a great way to exercise my lungs.

SPADIAMOND

Well, Pretty Lady, you keep up the exercising-------it looks good on you.

SPADIAMOND and NY LADY

(friendly laughter)

FOLEY

(running footsteps)

The LEVY TWINS (one twin sounds like a Bostonian and the other sounds like an Atlantan)

Mr. Spadiamond, hey there, Mr. Spadiamond

NY LADY

TAXI, TAXI!

FOLEY

(screeching of stopping taxi)

SPADIAMOND (and) LEVY TWINS

(Sounds of them colliding with each other)

SPADIAMOND

Whoa! girls, what's the big hurry?

LEVY TWINS (together with panting voices)

Gee whiz! Mr. Spadiamond, you just gotta help, Filmnoirville is in gr
eat, great big trouble.

FOLEY and EXTRAS

(sounds of aridfication, then traffic sounds & street crowd sounds)

SPADIAMOND

Let us get out of this din. We'll go get a booth at Tootsie's Diner.

Levy Twins

Can we get ice cream or a soda?

SPADIAMOND

Sure kids, why not.

MUSIC

(jukebox music fade-in)

~~LEVY TWINS~~

Levy Twins

Chocolate strawberry sundae and peanut butter praline soda and two spoons and two straws. No make that three spoons and three straws, gotta share with Mr. Spadiamond. (giggling)

SPADIAMOND

O.k., girls what's the big trouble for our fair city?

LEVY TWINS

The water, the water, the water.

SPADIAMOND

What water and what about it?

LEVY TWINS

The water tower will be empty in a couple of weeks.

FOLEY & EXTRAS

(s"ounds of dishes and silverware being placed on table, then slurping and ice cream eating sounds)

LEVY TWINS

Don't you get it Mr. Spadiamond? If there is no water ......

SPADIAMOND

EGADS! You're right, If there is no water we won't have that just -rained -on-ambience for which the streets of Filmnoirville are noted.

MUSIC (fade in)

ANNOUNCER (over music)

My! My! Ladies and Gentlemen what is a private detective to do. Can he and the Levy twins do anything to stop the ordinariness which is encroaching upon their light reflective streets of Filmnoirville? Tune in next week to find out if Filmnoirville is saved from the mundane dustiness of other cities; until then remember Blue Coal is the neighborly pollutant to warm your cozy home. Good night.

MUSIC (fades out)

COUSINS
by
The Godmoie

Cousins come in many forms. Some you get because your aunt or uncle have a baby. Some you get because your Nana and your Godmoie became friends around the age of twenty. Since then they shared good times and bad times. At some point early in your Nana's and your Godmoie's relationship, without words to each other, they chose to be friends for life. Thus far they have shared their friendship and families for over thirty-five years.

Over time family members have come and gone. Your Godmoie had her two babies in 1969 and 1970. Your Nana had her two babies in 1972 and 1975. These babies were treated by Nana and Godmoie as their nieces and nephew. So when the nieces and nephew had babies the cousinship continued.

Blood cousins and chosen cousins are all special and are all a joy to have and behold. Aunt Hollie and Uncle Rick have given you Jordan Davis as a blood cousin. Aunt Heather and Uncle Michael have given you Gabrielle Adaire, Emmalee Vendalia and Willoughbie Hannah Light as your chosen cousins.

No matter how you get them, cousins can be wonderful playmates and friends.

MISS HOLLIE JEAN
by
The Godmoie

Miss Hollie Jean
Ate a speckled jelly bean
Which made her opposite of fat.
Miss Hollie Jean
Found this situation NOT keen,
Because, what she wanted to be was a cat.

MEOW MEOW MEEOOW!

Miss Hollie Jean
Grew a tail of fur
And then grew fluffy ears.
Miss Hollie Jean
Acquired wispy white whiskers,
Which could help her hunt for years.

PURR PURR PUUURRR!

Miss Hollie Jean
Eventually got her wish:
For now she IS a cat.
Miss Hollie Jean
She laps her food from a cat dish.
So, what do you think of that?

HOW TO BECOME DAVEY CAKES
by
The Godmoie

Davey Cakes grew to be a man and a husband and a father but before that he was a baby, a boy and a kid.

It was a lovely summer's day and we all gathered at a church. It was the day the sweet baby boy would receive an additional set of parents. He would not live with the extra set of parents, but would be guided by them through his life. [At least that was the plan.]

As is tradition, the baby boy was handed over to the new Godmother. At that time the Godparents make promises before God and the attending church community to be there for the baby boy as he grows and matures.

Another important duty of the Godmother is to declare the name of the child to the officiating priest or pastor. Now at this point in the ritual the new Godmother was shy and unable to proclaim the name she really wanted to give the baby. She behaved in the expected way and when asked by the pastor the name of the child she said, "David William Appleby the third" - when what she wanted to say was, "I name this child Caleb Liam Seth Appleby the first."

Well, the truth is out, and no matter what name he is called by others, to his Godmother he has been her Davey Cakes. Don't you think for such a special Godson that his Godmother should have a special handle for the kid who is now a man. When he is fifty years old, he will still be her Davey Cakes. That's a promise.

THREE SISTERS
by
Moie

It was not long ago nor was it recently that a lady gave birth to three sisters. Much alike yet very different were these wee babes. Each had her own name and height and weight and birthdate, though they were all born in the same hospital.

The smallest was born first, weighing in at six pounds seven ounces, the next in line weighing in at seven pounds eight ounces; the youngest turned out to be the heaviest, weighing in at eight pounds nine ounces. Quite the trio were these bouncing baby sisters.

When the first sister was born, after many hours of trying to make her way out of the mother's birth canal, her Daddy could not take his eyes off of her, for she was the most beautiful baby he had ever seen. Because she took so long to come out and play, the first to feed her was her Daddy. The bottle was tiny, as was necessary for the tiny newborn.

Then almost two years later another lovely baby girl arrived to the family of three and that made four. This baby, as did the first, had to be induced to exit the mother's birth canal, but this baby made her escape from the birth canal more quickly than the first sister and this sister ate from the mother's breast very soon after she was born. As was the case with the first baby girl, all who gazed upon her were taken with her beauty.

Almost two years after the arrival of the second baby girl, the family grew from four members to five. Yes, another girl - and this girl was not induced. She came through the birth canal journey much more quickly than the two that had come before. She was the biggest and the hungriest, but just as pretty as her sisters. She also was the girl baby that looked most like the mommy.

Time has passed and these three sisters are pals and playmates to one another. They have had to endure some sad times, but mostly they enjoy happy times together. They are lucky and blessed to have each other to share their interesting lives. As they grow and their lives become more complicated they will always have a true and loving sisterhood, these three sisters.

DO YOU HAVE TO BE CANADIAN TO CATCH YOUR MAN?

by

TORI (SWAMP) LAKES

CAST OF CHARACTERS:
SAMUEL SHOVELLE ~ PRIVATE EYE #1
DICKY ZIRCONIUM ~ PRIVATE EYE #2
EFFIE FALSEHART ~ SECRETARY
MARGINAL STEWDIP ~ WOMAN
VANCE TALKELOT ~ ANNOUNCER
FOLEY ~ SOUND-FX PERSON

DO YOU HAVE TO BE CANADIAN TO CATCH YOUR MAN?

The 1999 retro-radio romp by
Tori Lakes
* * * * * * *

ANNOUNCER

Hello, radio friends. This is <u>Vance Talkelot</u> for "Do You Have To Be Canadian To Catch Your Man?", brought to you by LEG & ANVIL Baking Soda . . . the all-purpose powdery substance for everyone's home.

Yes, folks, LEG & ANVIL Baking Soda can soothe a baby's rashy bottom; it can take the sour smell from your kitchen drain; it can be made into a paste to extricate the stinger of a bee which has punctured your skin. And that's not all! Put LEG & ANVIL Baking Soda in your chocolate chip cookie batter, and . . . Yuuuummmmmm!

So, ladies, the next time you visit your local market, don't forget to put LEG & ANVIL Baking Soda on your shopping list. Remember, the all-purpose powdery substance for everyone's home is . . . LEG & ANVIL Baking Soda.

Now, let us listen in as our favorite secretary, Effie Falsehart, converses with a potential client for her bosses.

EFFIE
[on the phone]
Un-huh . . . That's correct . . . We have an appointment open at 1:45 this afternoon with P.I. Shovelle, or at 1:55 if you wish to see both Shovelle and Zirconium. . . Fine, we'll see you then.

FOLEY: _Door opens; trumpet music from the office radio statics in and out._

SAMUEL & DICKY _are humming to the trumpet music_

EFFIE
Better take a short lunch today.

DICKY
Why's that, Honeybun?

EFFIE
You'd better make sure you have your sports jackets.

SAMUEL
Like he said, why's that, Honeybun?

EFFIE
A client!!

FOLEY: _Sounds of DICKY & SAMUEL dancing_

SAMUEL & DICKY
[singing in unison]
"We're in the mo-ney , da do dado -
Hap-py days are here again"

FOLEY: *Sounds of <u>tires</u> <u>screeching</u>* - then - *<u>crash</u>*

DICKY

Honeybun, call the police. They will want to untangle that mess in the street.

EFFIE

Already doing it, Mr Zirconium.

SAMUEL

Yeah, Mr Zirconium, our Honeybun is already ringing the coppers.

FOLEY: *More <u>tire</u> <u>screeching</u>* - then - *a <u>siren</u>*

DICKY

Boy, that was quick.

SAMUEL

There's that new donut shop at the end of the block; guess the coppers . . .

DICKY

You betcha, Sammy me boy, our boys in blue will be decorated with powdered sugar and a dab or two of jelly to add a bit of contrasting color.

FOLEY: *Phone <u>rings</u>*

EFFIE
[answering the phone]
Shovelle & Zirconium, Private Detectives. How may I help you?

DICKY

Look at her, Sammy. 'Tis our Effie of Honeybun, a delight for the eyes, as she speaks for us into the receiver.

EFFIE

[still on the phone]

I'm sorry, madame, but the soonest either of our operatives could meet with you would be . . .

FOLEY: *Knock at office door*

DICKY

[in his best John Barrymore voice]

ENTER!

EFFIE

[continuing on the phone]

. . . Thursday at eleven A.M. . . . No, I'm sorry, but if a cancellation occurs I will call you . . . Yes, madame . . . Your number . . . was that 4659? . . . Very well . . . You're welcome.

FOLEY: *Sound of receiver being placed on its cradle* - then -
        Trumpet on the radio blows its final note

SAMUEL

If I heard my Honeybun correctly, it's time for an encore!

FOLEY: *Dancing sounds*

SAMUEL & DICKY

[singing in unison]

"We're in the mo-ney - That's so, my Honey - Cuz hap-py days are here again"

SAMUEL & DICKY & EFFIE
[they all laugh]
[then they all speak in unison]

A-nother client!!

EFFIE

Donuts, anyone? On you, of course.

Ms STEWDIP
[at the door]

Excuse me!

SAMUEL & DICKY & EFFIE

Yes. May we help you?

Ms STEWDIP
[still at the door]

I need help.

DICKY

Help is what we do, Ms . . . ?

Ms STEWDIP

Stewdip . . . Marginal Stewdip

EFFIE

Ms Stewdip, won't you come this way?

FOLEY: *sound of high heels walking & bangle bracelets tinging*
- then - a THUD

Ms STEWDIP

My goodness. What was that?

EFFIE

Not to worry. It's just the sound my employers make when they think.

Ms STEWDIP

Pardon me?

EFFIE

Oh, did I say that out loud?

FOLEY: *sound of male shoes entering the inner office*

DICKY

Ms Falsehart, will you take the call on line two?

FOLEY: *sound of high heels leaving the room*

SAMUEL

Marginal Stewdip - umm - Do you have a relative named Dizzy?

Ms STEWDIP

Yes, sir. He's my brother, Rupert; but he goes by Dizzy. Actually it is because of him that I need your help.

DICKY

Is your brother experiencing some difficulty?

Ms STEWDIP
[through bursting boo-hoos]

He has stolen something. I don't know what it is, but St. Louis is up in arms over this theft. [boo-hoos] But the odd thing is, the theft occurred in Cincinnati. And the inhabitants of the Queen City are not at all upset.

SAMUEL

Where is your brother now?

Ms STEWDIP

He is hitch-hiking through western Europe.

DICKY

Are you able to contact him while he's maneuvering the terra firma across the Big Pond?

Ms STEWDIP

No, that's why I have come to you. I hope you can find out what he has stolen and perhaps return it to the city of St. Louis.

FOLEY: *Buzzer sounds once*

SAMUEL
[responding to buzzer]

Yes?

EFFIE

Your next appointment is here.

SANDY'S BOY
by
TORI LAKES FREEDMAN

All babies are born through what is called the birth canal, unless of course they come out the zipper way on the mother's belly.

Not all mommys get their babies that way. Some mommys just choose a baby. That's what my Mommy did.

I'm not sure how she found me, but I think my Mommy's mommy helped her. See, my Mommy's mommy was up in Heaven and I think she saw me before I was sent down that birth canal thing.

Anyway, I never really met my Mommy's mommy because I was just a baby and I don't remember much before my coming out party. Actually my real coming out party started when my Mommy found me.

I am so glad she did, because sometimes things are so confusing when the world starts making a lot of noise.

My Mommy and I are a lot alike and a lot different from each other.

First, she is a girl and I am not. She is tall and I am short. She is G-or-g-eous [like that handsome man Benjamin Bratt who played an FBI agent] in one of Mommy's work things. Oh! I am G-or-g-eous also, just look at me.

Mommy's hair is dark, fine and usually straight. My hair is dark and curly. She likes my hair best.

Did I tell you that we have one thing in common? We like people. We like caramel colored people, we like dark chocolate colored people, we like peach people, we probably like green people _ _ but I haven't seen any of them in real life. Sometimes you might see green people in Mommy's work type thingys.

When you go to the grocery store with your mommy, do people come up and talk to her? I mean a whole mess of people. Well, that happens to us. They are nice people, they just really like my Mommy. I mean really, really like her. Sometimes they are so happy they cry. Sometimes they try to talk but words just can not make it out of their mouths.

It's so funny, there was this one guy who kept purposely tripping himself. He said it was an homage to Gracie somebody. Mommy just smiled and told him he never had to do that again. I still laugh when I think about that guy!

Oh! Do people always want to take their picture with your mommy? They do with mine. She is nice about it, but she says, "Yes, that would be nice, but not of my son." They are usually understanding, yet there are those nasty people who call out her name thinking she will turn in their direction. And if they don't get what they call the shot they want they sometimes become disrespectful.

I don't like it when people are disrespectful to my Mommy. Mommy is really big on being respectful!! That's a good thing, yes it is!

THE END

TORI'S RADIO PLAY - XMAS 2001   *by Tori Lakes Freedman*
CAST OF CHARACTERS
===

ANNOUNCER

SPADIAMOND

NEW YORK BAR LADY

CLAMMY HANDS GUY

THE LEVY TWINS (Girls: one sounds like a Bostonian and the other sounds like an Atlantan. They speak in unison or every other word or however the actors decide.)

EXTRAS (Whoever's not busy at the time)

FOLEY:
> foot steps and cheerful whistling
> sounds of claw pulling from skirt
> sounds of Clammy Hands Man getting up from the pavement
> street noise over the good-byes
> sounds of Clammy Hands Man walking away
> running footsteps
> screeching of stopping taxi
> aridfication
> traffic sounds
> sounds of dishes and silverware being placed on table

MUSIC:
> Theme music
> songs and singing drifting from the bars
> juke box music in soda shop
****

|
',"'TORI'S RADIO PLAY - XMAS 2001
===
ANNOUNCER

Good day ladies and gentlemen and welcome to the first installment of soon to be your favorite private detective, Samuel Richard Spadiamond, brought to you by Blue Coal. There's a good warm feeling from the glow of Blue Coal as well as the satisfaction of knowing that it helps to create the refreshing acid rain that exfoliates the deciduous and evergreen trees down wind of your home town.^ So tonight at bath time crank up that heat and feel good that you are keeping your neighbors down wind of you from having to rake up those pesky autumn leaves. Blue Coal is the neighborly heating product, use it in good health. (cough,cough, cough)

Music

(THEME MUSIC FOR SHOW)

ANNOUNCER

AND NOW WITH NO FURTHER DELAY BLUE COAL BRINGS TO YOU, SAMUEL RICHARD SPADIAMOND, P.I.

FOLEY

(foot steps and cheerful whistling)

SPADIAMOND

It's quite relaxing to walk the streets of Filmnoirville in the late evening with the flickering of the neon lights and the smell of booze oozing from the beer joints, stepping over the odd tipsilated ejected bar patron, tipping one's fedora at the loveÙly leggy ladies....

NEW YORK BAR LADY

HEY! Mister, what do you think you're doin'? Keep your clammy hands to yourself.

CLAMMY HANDS GUY

Sorry, kid, seems my claw is caught on your nicely fitting straight skirt hem.
If you could just stand still I can try to detangle the SITuation.

NEW YORK LADY

Say! You pulling my leg or what?

CLAMMY HANDS GUY

Nah! Just trying to keep your threads intact.

SPADIAMOND

Hello there pretty lady, What are you and Clammy up to? Didn't know that you two where acquainted.

NY LADY

We ain't acquainted, we're attached.

SPADIAMOND

When's the big day?

145

NY LADY

What?

CLAMMY HANDS GUY

Hey, kid, hold still. Nothing is going to disattach unless you quit your squirming. Know what I mean?

FOLEY

(Traffic noises)

MUSIC

(songs and singing drifting from the bars)

EXTRAS

(mumblings of conversation of passers-by)

SPADIAMOND

Where's the honeymoon going to be?

NY LADY

Sammy Dick, are you drunk? I can't make any sense of what you are saying and why don't you get this guy off of me...

CLAMMY HANDS GUY

Look kid, if you don't do the cooperation thing your skirt is a gonner! And not only that....

NY LADY

Let go of my skirt, mister, or I'll have my USED to be friend here wallop you up along side of your head and if.....

Clammy HANDS GUY

P.I. man, is that you up there?

SPADIAMOND

How's things Clammy?

CLAMMY HANDS GUY

Could be worse, the caterpillar turned into a butterfly last week and flew the coop.

NY LADY

IF YOU TWO ARE FINISHED CATCHING UP ON THE DAY'S NEWS!!!!

SPADIAMOND and CLAMMY HANDS GUY

(in unison) Unh? What?

CLAMMY HANDS GUY

P.I. man, give me a hand here. I'm all tangled up in this kid's skirt.

SPADIAMOND

GOTCHA! Hey, pretty lady, Clammy here is stuck to your skirt and he needs you to hold still.
Here let me hold on to you until....

FOLEY

(sounds of claw pulling from skirt)

NY LADY

Oh, Sammy Dick. What a relief, I thought this guy was trying to get fresh.

SPADIAMOND

Pretty Lady, I'd like to introduce to you CLAMMY, a gentleman of integrity and good will, not to
mention a man of unusual handage.

FOLEY

(sounds of Clammy getting up from the pavement)

NY LADY

OOOhhh! Mr. Clammy, can you forgive my rudeness of misunderstanding?

CLAMMY HANDS GUY

No problem kid, already forgotten. Say P.I.man, you joining the crowd at Murphy O'Shea's next
week?

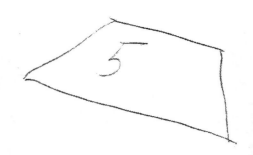

SPADIAMOND

Wouldn't miss it, Clammy my man, wouldn't miss it.

FOLEY

(street noise over the good-byes)

CLAMMY HANDS MAN

Catch you later P.I.man.   Unusual meeting you, kid.

FOLEY

(sounds of Clammy walking away)

EXTRAS

(street crowd mumblings)

SPADIAMOND

It's too noisy out here; let's pop into Franky's for a tall cool one.

NY LADY

No can do, Sammy Dick, I'm on my way to choir practice.

SPADIAMOND

Didn't know you were a church regular.

NY LADY

I'm not. I am a choir practice regular; it's a great way to exercise my lungs.

SPADIAMOND

Well, Pretty Lady, you keep up the exercising-------it looks good on you.

SPADIAMOND and NY LADY

(friendly laughter)

FOLEY

(running footsteps)

The LEVY TWINS (one twin sounds like a Bostonian and the other sounds like an Atlantan)

Mr. Spadiamond, hey there, Mr. Spadiamond

NY LADY

TAXI, TAXI!

FOLEY

(screeching of stopping taxi)

SPADIAMOND (and) LEVY TWINS

(Sounds of them colliding with each other)

SPADIAMOND

Whoa! girls, what's the big hurry?

LEVY TWINS (together with panting voices)

Gee whiz! Mr. Spadiamond, you just gotta help, Filmnoirville is in gr
eat, great big trouble.

FOLEY and EXTRAS

(sounds of aridfication, then traffic sounds & street crowd sounds)

SPADIAMOND

Let us get out of this din. We'll go get a booth at Tootsie's Diner.

Levy Twins

Can we get ice cream or a soda?

SPADIAMOND

Sure kids, why not.

MUSIC

(jukebox music fade-in)

LEVY TWINS

149

Levy Twins

Chocolate strawberry sundae and peanut butter praline soda and two spoons and two straws. No make that three spoons and three straws, gotta share with Mr. Spadiamond. (giggling)

SPADIAMOND

O.k., girls what's the big trouble for our fair city?

LEVY TWINS

The water, the water, the water.

SPADIAMOND

What water and what about it?

LEVY TWINS

The water tower will be empty in a couple of weeks.

FOLEY & EXTRAS

(s"ounds of dishes and silverware being placed on table, then slurping and ice cream eating sounds)

LEVY TWINS

Don't you get it Mr. Spadiamond? If there is no water ......

SPADIAMOND

EGADS! You're right, If there is no water we won't have that just -rained -on-ambience for which the streets of Filmnoirville are noted.

MUSIC (fade in)

ANNOUNCER (over music)

My! My! Ladies and Gentlemen what is a private detective to do. Can he and the Levy twins do anything to stop the ordinariness which is encroaching upon their light reflective streets of Filmnoirville? Tune in next week to find out if Filmnoirville is saved from the mundane dustiness of other cities; until then remember Blue Coal is the neighborly pollutant to warm your cozy home. Good night.

MUSIC (fades out)

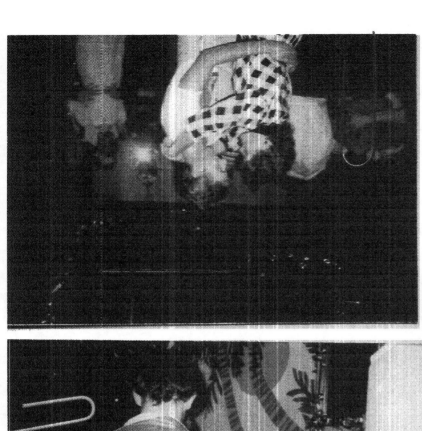

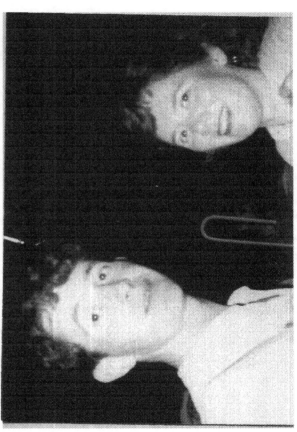

Rich & Heather
at Shenita's Disco
July, 84

Mom & Patty
Shander's disco
July, 84

Brian & Kelli
Shander's disco
July, 84

The disco
July, 84

THE IRISH ROVERS

Bill Girdwood, Booking / Production Manager

1720 Cypress Point, Ct

Pahrump, NV, 89048

Cell: 775-764-1371

shamey shamey song thanks / shame on ye!

They kinda started it, back in, late 1975 and
Before April of 1976. Front Row Theatre,

— Highland Heights . O.H.I.O (Tim Conway from that
   area became Tom Conway
— Pointer Sisters/nice ladies,   due to! in the unions,
   BIG Redneck story about   there already was a Tom C
   their time at →
— Bob Freedman, everyone with the 1976 H.B. Tour
except Harry & ?

– Kate Smith = Kind – Waylon ~~Jenny~~ Jennings = long legs
had to step over
them – Smiley!

– Burt Bacharach w/ Anthony Newley) Total fun, A' gentle MAN.

total Jack ASS (Donkey is another word)

they are the same animal

– A (trucker) of Some Sort = Crude = asked me
" Do you Know What I would like you to do for ME,"
said the Rucker. My mouth said, "What's that sir?"

– He proceded to tell me → ✗ I proceeded
to the lovely Lady who showed diners to their
seats – Holey Moley! I WAS 28 yrs.

– ~~Dion Warwick~~ Dionne Warwick : Sat at the bar far
end ~~from~~ 'BAR' entrance. Nobody bothered her. Quiet &
pensive.

– Two ~~wis~~ wise guys : I do appreciate their Kindness
↘ at a 2 person table essentially (bar area/between.) I dropped
the ✗ Huge tray (I'm 5' & all of 105 lbs. at that time)

= Fish No longer
on plate or tray.
Tray on Floor – how
oops WAS I hot (didn't)

→ reside on said floor,
My own five & self = Irish
GENES – ¯ –

Big tip — New Fish — Big Smiles = (So Happy too)
old Burt ~~snot~~ Snobbach WASN't there also
– Used SLA = ? skills / Thanks Koko

I WAS ONLY on Staff From Dec. 1975 to MAY 3RD
or 5th
1976

Started and finished on a typewriter, 1977

at 125
East 82ND
Apt. B
N.Y.C.
Next to THE
CHURCH

Of Whom Is Your Tree More Fond?

by

Victoria Lakes Freedman

Once upon a time, in a town much the same as yours, lived two sisters, Vendalia and Delonia.

Vendalia had the most beautiful blue eyes you could ever imagine. Her hair was dark brown, with just a hint of curl in it.

Delonia had nice eyes, too. They were not as big as Vendalia's eyes, and the blue was not quite as deep. But her hair had many lovely shades of blonde, all coming together to form beautiful golden curls.

Vendalia and Delonia loved each other very much, as well they should. They both loved their mother and each sister wanted Mother to love her the most. They were constantly competing with each other for Mother's love.

Now . . . If you are very quiet and pay close attention, you will hear all about a great adventure that these girls recently experienced.

It started one summer's evening, not long after suppertime. The sun had just set, and the two sisters were in their back yard watching the bright flashes of fireflies.

"Vendalia and Delonia, it is time to come inside," called the girls' mother from the back door.

"Coming, Mother," said the girls in unison.

Once inside, the girls took their baths, dried themselves and put on their frilly summer pyjamas.

As they were getting ready to climb into bed, Vendalia asked, "Mother, do you love me the most?" Before Mother could answer, Delonia ran up to her and whined, "No, Mother loves *me* the most."

"Girls, please come here, sit down and listen," said Mother, as she patted the bed on either side of her. "We have had this discussion many times before, haven't we?"

Both of the girls nodded silently.

Mother said, "I love you both very much, each in a very special way. I love you not only because you are my children, but also because you are both very nice little people. Love is not to be measured. It is to be shared among those who love each other.

"Do you understand what I am telling you?"

"Yes, Mother," said Vendalia as she threw her arms around Mother's neck.

"I think I understand, too, Mother," said Delonia. "It's like when you have two pets and you love them both very much and if one gets hurt you pay more attention to that one, right?"

"Well, Delonia, you are starting to get the idea, but it is not quite that simple," replied Mother. "Right now it is bedtime, my darlings. How about our special lullaby tonight?"

"Yeah, that's a good idea," yelled Delonia.

"O.K., girls, lie down, close your eyes and get comfortable," said Mother. She began singing the lullaby, watching Vendalia and Delonia ease into a relaxing sleep.

After a while, Vendalia began to stir and opened her eyes just a slit. She opened and closed her eyes several times as if she couldn't believe what she saw. Sitting up in her bed and opening her eyes again, she looked carefully around. There was deep green grass, spotted with many kinds of flowers and trees, as far as her eyes could see. The sky was a clear light blue, laced with fluffy white clouds.

"This isn't our room. Where are we?" mumbled the dark-haired girl to herself.

Once again Vendalia blinked her eyes to make sure she was seeing what she thought she was seeing. Then she leaned over and shook her blonde sister. "Wake up, Delonia, you won't believe what has happened."

In her crabby morning voice Delonia said, "I don't want to wake up. Leave me alone or I'll call Mother."

"Mother isn't here, Delonia. We aren't home"

"What do you mean?" Delonia opened her eyes and at once she knew Vendalia was telling her the truth. "Wow, how beautiful!"

"Come on, Delonia, let's get out of bed and look around. Maybe we can find some breakfast," suggested Vendalia. "Come over here, by this banana tree. Here are two bowls of cereal with bananas in them."

"I just found two glasses of orange juice over there," Delonia answered, as she pointed toward an orange tree.

The girls enjoyed a tasty breakfast in this land in which they had awakened.

"Are you finished yet, Vendalia?" questioned Delonia.

Vendalia replies, "Yes, I am. Let's look around."

Just then a deep voice boomed, "Wait just a minute."

"Why? And what's wrong with your voice, Delonia?" snapped Vendalia.

"That wasn't me," snarled Delonia. "And if it wasn't you, then it was nobody, because all I can see is you and me."

"It was I!" proudly proclaimed a man made of grass, as he rose up from his spot on the lawn. The grass man continued, "I never saw you two little girls before."

At this point both girls were a bit frightened. Since Vendalia was the older, she stood protectively in front of Delonia and said, "My name is Vendalia and this is my younger sister, Delonia. What is your name?"

"My name? I don't know." The grass man seemed confused. "No one or no thing has ever asked me that before."

"That's silly. Everyone has a name," said Delonia with a frown forming across her brow. "You get a name when you are born."

"I have not been born and I am not a person."

"No, you are grass," Vendalia chuckled, "but you have been born. You sprouted up through the soil from seeds into many blades of grass." Vendalia threw up her arms as an encouraging gesture. "Now all you need is for someone to give you a name, or name yourself."

"Gee! Vendalia, I didn't know you were so smart," Delonia said with new-found pride in her dark-haired sister.

"Thanks for the compliment, but now is the time for us to give our green friend a name or at least help him think of a name for himself."

"Golly, girls, I just can't think of any name for myself," the green grass man said with dewy tears beginning to form in his grassy eyes.

Delonia tried to comfort him. "Don't cry, sir. I'll give you a name. How about Jasper?"

"Jasper," repeated the grass man to himself. "That's a marvelous name.

"Please allow me to introduce myself," the grass man said, bowing gracefully toward the girls. "My name is Jasper."

The girls laughed and jumped up and down joyfully with their new friend, Jasper, who just happened to be a green grass man.

They all formed a circle and shouted out one letter at a time, as in a cheer:

J - A - S - P - E - R

J - A - S - P - E - R

J - A - S - P - E - R

Jasper   Jasper   Jasper

YEAAAAAAAAAAAAH!!!

"Thank you both very much for caring enough about me to give me a name," said Jasper shyly. The sisters could tell that he was embarrassed by the way his green grass cheeks became just a bit red around the edges.

"Jasper," questioned Vendalia, "why did you ask us to wait?"

"Oh! All this excitement made me forget. I told you to wait because you were leaving your dirty breakfast dishes on the ground."

"That's right," remarked Delonia. "We know we should put things away when we are finished with them. But Mother always washes our dishes. We just put them in the sink."

"Well, I don't see your mother here, so you girls will have to take care of the washing yourselves."

Vendalia said, "I don't see a sink anywhere, so we will just have to find a stream to wash these dishes in."

"Very good thinking." Jasper nodded his approval. "And I shall accompany you to the stream."

The girls gathered up the bowls, the spoons and the juice glasses. Then the trio walked through the field, crossed a path, and went to the bottom of a hill. There they came to a clear, gently running stream.

There were signs along the side of the stream with instructions on them.

"No dish-washing here. Go downstream," proclaimed the first sign.

"This spot for watering lawn," said the second one.

"Go upstream to bathe people," added the third.

"Bird bath temporarily out of birds," announced the fourth.

The last sign read, "Follow this arrow for further instructions."

"Girls, since we are so close to the lawn-watering spot, would you mind helping me get watered?" asked Jasper.

"Of course we will help you," replied Delonia.

"Well then," said Jasper, "lets go down by the edge of the stream. Delonia, if you let me put my head on your lap while Vendalia splashes water on me from the stream, I shall be most appreciative."

"Jasper," asked Vendalia with a puzzled look on her face, "why don't you just get into the water?"

Jasper started laughing, "I can't swim. Did you ever see a green grass man swim?"

"I can't say that I have. But I never heard a patch of lawn talk before, either," remarked Vendalia sarcastically.

After helping Jasper get watered, the two sisters grew tired and decided to take a nap.

When they awoke they were all alone, but there was a new sign which read, "Goodbye, Vendalia and Delonia. I had to go back to my spot. HAVE A HAPPY DAY. Your friend, Jasper."

"Wasn't that weird, Vendalia! We actually carried on a conversation with a patch of lawn."

"Yeah, I can't wait to tell Mother."

"I get to tell her first, Vendalia," Delonia said with anger.

"You always want to tell Mother first. You're such a baby, Delonia."

"I am not a baby! Don't call me names," pouted Delonia. "Anyway, Vendalia, we still have to wash these dishes."

"O.K., come on. There are some arrows pointing to the dish-washing area," says Vendalia.

Soon the girls found the dish-washing area and carefully cleaned the bowls, the spoons and the juice glasses.

As they set off to return the dishes to where they had found them, a Y-shaped branch began to chant, "The big tree is more fond of me. The big tree is more fond of me." The branch was standing alone, about five feet from the sisters.

"Mister Branch, why do you keep saying, 'The big tree is more fond of me'?", questioned Delonia.

"Don't be silly, little girl, the big tree is more fond of me , not you !" responded the branch.

"My sister knows what you mean," said Vendalia protectively. "Anyway, why is the big tree more fond of you, Mister Branch?"

"Because I am the best branch my tree has," Mister Branch boasted. "I am the strongest and the prettiest. And when the wind blows I sway better than any of the other branches. Which one of you does your tree like best?"

Vendalia and Delonia both laughed very loudly. Finally they realized that Mister Branch did not find any humor in the question he had put to them.

Delonia said, "Oh, Mister Branch, we don't have a tree. That is to say, we do have trees but not like you mean."

"You do have a tree. You don't have a tree," snarled Mister Branch. "It sounds as though you don't know what you have. You speak like those other branches my tree has. . . stupidly."

"Now hold on there, Mister Branch. There is no need to be rude to my sister," snapped Vendalia. "She was trying to clarify something to you, something of which you were ignorant."

"Wow, Vendalia, you sure know some big words," whispered Delonia. Then she raised her voice and said to Mister Branch, "What I was trying to explain to you was that Vendalia and I are people. We have a mother that watches over us, not a tree. When I said that we have trees, I meant out in our yard." Finally Delonia asks, "Do you understand, Mister Branch?"

"I suppose so," answered Mister Branch sullenly, "but you see, I never met any people before. My tree has talked about people a few times. My brother branch, Earl, said that he had met some people once, but he didn't like them."

"Well, Mister Branch, now you have met people, too. My name is Vendalia and this is my sister, Delonia. We are pleased to make your acquaintance and we hope that you will like us."

The girls both smiled and bowed their heads slightly to show respect. Then Delonia asked, "What is your name? You do have a name, don't you? Of course you wouldn't have to have a name. We met a green grass man earlier today and he didn't have a name until we gave him one."

"Oh, but I do have a name," answered Mister Branch proudly. "My name is Sherman."

"What a fine name that is," Vendalia says.

"Certainly Sherman is a fine name," angrily retorted the Y-shaped branch. "I would not have anything but the finest name. I would never admit to having a name such as yours, Vendalia. It is so ugly."

At hearing this, Delonia became very angry.

"Don't listen to him, Vendalia. He's not very nice.

"Now look what you have done, Sherman. You have hurt Vendalia's feelings."

"Who cares?" replied Sherman. "I don't have time to fool around with you touchy people."

Sherman walked away from the girls mumbling to himself, "Earl is right. People are not likeable. But of course, neither is Earl."

Soon Sherman had moved out of sight of the girls. Delonia was still trying to cheer Vendalia, when the sisters heard the sound of quiet sobbing.

"My goodness, someone is very sad," sniffed Vendalia as she wiped the tears from her eyes.

"Maybe we can help," urged Delonia. "Come on the sobbing is coming from behind that large rock."

The girls walked to the other side of the large rock only to find a garden. Somehow, this garden seemed different from any garden that Vendalia and Delonia had ever seen before.

Suddenly, the girls heard a tiny shrill voice saying, "How do you do?"

While looking around for the owner of the voice, Vendalia answered, "We do quite nicely, thank you."

Again the tiny voice spoke. "May I help you?"

Delonia looked down and giggled. "Why, you're a carrot. A talking carrot!"

"Well, Delonia," muttered Vendalia, grinning. "Why not? We have heard a patch of lawn talk and we have heard a tree branch talk."

As politely as possible, the carrot interrupted. "Did I hear you correctly? Did you say that you have heard a tree branch and a patch of lawn talk?"

"That's right," replied the sisters, in unison.

"Well, I find that absolutely mind-boggling," the carrot said with astonishment.

"Meaning no offense, but hearing a carrot speak is a bit mind-boggling to us," responded Vendalia.

"Now that puzzles me, young ladies, for I am a vegetable. And it is commonly known that vegetables speak. Why," sighs the carrot, "how else would I communicate?

"Well, never mind about that now. I have neglected my manners. Once again, how do you do, ladies? My name is Felix. Welcome to our garden."

"Thank you, Felix. My name is Vendalia."

"And I am Delonia. We are sisters," Delonia said as she pointed to Vendalia.

"What brought you to our garden?" asked Felix.

Delonia replied quickly, "We heard someone crying and thought we might be able to help."

"Oh, how very kind of you. But not to worry," said Felix. "That was Madame Potato you heard. She always cries her eyes out when Sir Onion gets near her. He is such a cutup, you see."

Vendalia and Delonia began laughing at what Felix had just told them. They laughed so hard and long that tears dribbled down their cheeks. As this was happening, Sir Onion walked toward the trio so he could meet the visitors.

Felix the carrot told Sir Onion what had brought the young ladies to their garden. Then he introduced Sir Onion to the girls.

"You see, ladies," remarked Sir Onion, "you have just met me and already you are crying. Now you can imagine how Madame Potato feels."

"Did I hear my name mentioned?" sang out Madame Potato as she rolled up to the group. "My, my, what have we here? These girls are such adorable little creatures, aren't they?"

Felix interjected, "Madame Potato, if you could settle down for a second I would gladly introduce you to them."

"Certainly, Felix, I would like that. But you keep your distance, Sir Onion, so that I can keep my eyes dry."

Felix the carrot introduced Vendalia and Delonia to Madame Potato, after which he told Madame Potato why the girls had come to the garden.

"Ladies, I am disappointed that you are not able to join us. Maybe another time," Felix said graciously. "It has been delightful chatting with both of you. I must say good-bye until we meet again."

"That goes for me, too," chimed in Madame Potato. "I surely hope you sweet things stop back here again sometime." When the large Potato rolled clumsily away, Vendalia and Delonia walked back to the dish-washing area.

"I think we should try going back the same way we came," suggested Vendalia to her blond sister.

Delonia asked, "Do you mean to the place where we found the dishes this morning?"

"Yes" answered Vendalia. "So if you carry the bowls, I will carry the juice glasses and the spoons."

The girls strolled by the edge of the stream. It was not long before they were back to the area where they had last seen Jasper.

"Vendalia, I am afraid. We have been here a long time and Mother hasn't come looking for us," sobs Delonia.

"Don't cry, Delonia," comforts Vendalia. "You'll see. We will be home before you know it. Anyway, I don't think Mother knows about this place."

"You're a nice sister, Vendalia. Now I can understand why Mother loves you the most."

"That's a coincidence, Delonia, because I was just thinking the same thing about you."

"Ladies, I am disappointed that you are not able to join us. Maybe another time," Felix said graciously. "It has been delightful chatting with both of you. I must say good-bye until we meet again."

"That goes for me, too," chimed in Madame Potato. "I surely hope you sweet things stop back here again sometime." When the large Potato rolled clumsily away, Vendalia and Delonia walked back to the dish-washing area.

"I think we should try going back the same way we came," suggested Vendalia to her blond sister.

Delonia asked, "Do you mean to the place where we found the dishes this morning?"

"Yes" answered Vendalia. "So if you carry the bowls, I will carry the juice glasses and the spoons."

The girls strolled by the edge of the stream. It was not long before they were back to the area where they had last seen Jasper.

"Vendalia, I am afraid. We have been here a long time and Mother hasn't come looking for us," sobs Delonia.

"Don't cry, Delonia," comforts Vendalia. "You'll see. We will be home before you know it. Anyway, I don't think Mother knows about this place."

"You're a nice sister, Vendalia. Now I can understand why Mother loves you the most."

"That's a coincidence, Delonia, because I was just thinking the same thing about you."

By this time the girls had climbed the hill and were about to cross the path.

"Vendalia, look. Isn't that Sherman?"

"My goodness, it looks like he is hurt."

Neither Vendalia nor Delonia said another word. They just ran in the direction of Sherman as fast as their little legs would carry them.

A bit out of breath, the girls said in unison, "Sherman, what happened?"

"I am so glad to see you. Will you help me?" begs Sherman. "My limb is broken."

"Of course," says Delonia. "What can we do?"

Sherman replies, "Thank you, thank you. I am not worthy of your help. Please forgive me, Vendalia. I don't know why I get so arrogant. Please, Vendalia."

Vendalia interrupts, "Stop worrying, Sherman, I forgive you. Now let us help you."

Delonia asks Vendalia, "Can you tie this ribbon around the broken part? If you can, I will hold his limb straight."

"Is what we plan to do all right with you, Sherman?" asks Delonia.

"Yes, but please hurry. I want to go home to my tree," complains Sherman.

Delonia straightened Sherman's limb and Vendalia secured the ribbon around the break.

"O.K., Sherman, we are finished. Now let's get you to your tree," suggests Vendalia.

Suddenly Sherman began crying profusely.

"Are you in a lot of pain, Sherman?" asks Vendalia.

"No, I just realized something terrible," sobs Sherman.

Delonia says, "Sherman, if you're not in pain, then there is nothing to worry about."

"Yes there is," Sherman continued to sob. "I am no longer the strongest or the prettiest branch my tree has. And worse than that, I won't be able to sway better. At least not until my limb heals."

Vendalia gently scolded Sherman. "You are being very silly and babyish. Sure, you can't sway now. But once you heal you will sway as well as ever. Even better."

Sherman was not consoled. "But my tree will no longer be more fond of me."

At hearing this, the girls realized how wrong they had been about their own mother's love.

"Come on, Sherman, stop crying and let's get you home," said Delonia. "You put Sherman's leafy right limb around your neck, Vendalia, and I'll put his leafy left limb around my neck. Then we will carry him. He is not too heavy."

Before long the sisters had returned Sherman home to his tree.

"Oh my dear Sherman, what has happened to my little branch?" questioned the tree.

"I was on my way home when I tripped over a rock. When I fell, my limb cracked," answered Sherman. "These are my new friends, Vendalia and Delonia. They found me and fixed my limb with this ribbon. Then they carried me all the way home."

"Thank you," said the tree as she took Sherman into her limbs. "How can I ever thank you enough?"

"We're happy that we were able to help, aren't we, Delonia?"

Delonia nodded in agreement.

"Girls, come rest while I make Sherman comfortable."

"Just for a minute," said Vendalia. "We have to get home soon."

"Oh, Vendalia," whispered Delonia. "We forgot the dishes."

"That's right, we left them where we found Sherman."

"Don't worry, girls," Sherman's tree said. "I will send one of Sherman's sibling branches to fetch them for you."

After making Sherman the branch comfortable, the tree talked with Vendalia and Delonia. "It will take Earl a few minutes to get back with the dishes. Then you can be on your way home.

"How did you meet Sherman?" inquired the tree.

The girls told the tree all about their meeting. They also told her that Sherman thought she would not be as fond of him now.

"Oh, that dear Sherman," sighed the tree. "He gets strange ideas. You know he wants to think that I am more fond of him than I am of my other branches."

"Yes, we know," replied Delonia. "He talks about it a lot."

"If only Sherman could realize that I am equally fond of all my branches. As far as my feelings are concerned," Sherman's tree continued, "there is no need for his competitiveness.

"Vendalia, do you feel that your tree – I mean your mother, of course – is more fond of you?"

"No, but sometimes I wish she were," replied Vendalia.

"I have felt that way, too," added Delonia, "but now I know that it isn't important for Mother to love me the most."

"Delonia is right," Vendalia agreed. "What is important is that we know our mother loves both of us very much."

"Your mother is a very fortunate person to have such bright young girls as daughters," remarked Sherman's tree.

Just then Sherman's brother branch, Earl, arrived. "Here are the bowls, spoons and glasses you sent me after," he said, somewhat out of breath.

"Thank you very much, Earl," said Vendalia. Each of the sisters took a bowl, a spoon and a juice glass from the branch.

Delonia added, "Yes, thank you, Earl. I guess we should be going now."

"Oh dear! I don't know how we get back there from here," declared Vendalia.

"Tell me, girls, did you get those dishes by a banana tree and an orange tree?" asked Sherman's tree.

"Yes, we did," Delonia shouted with relief.

"Then there is no problem," said Sherman's tree. "All you have to do is walk along side of the daisies. They form a trail between the orange tree and the banana tree."

"Well, that sounds simple enough, but how do we find the daisies?" asked Vendalia.

Sherman's tree said, "Do you see that row of peach trees over there?"

Vendalia and Delonia nodded their heads.

Sherman's tree continued, "Once you reach the peach trees, turn right. Then follow the row until it crosses the daisy trail. Then turn left at the daisy trail and soon you will arrive at your destination."

"Thank you for your help. Please tell Sherman that we said good-bye," Vendalia called out as she and Delonia started hurrying toward the peach trees.

Just before the girls reached the peach trees they turned and waved a final farewell to the tree family.

"You know, Vendalia, I am really getting tired. Aren't you?"

"Yes, I am tired, too, Delonia, but we shouldn't rest until we return these dishes. Better yet, we should wait until we get home."

"I suppose you're right," Delonia sighed wearily.

"Delonia," Vendalia exclaimed with excitement, "there's the daisy trail."

"Hurray! We shouldn't have much further to go," yelled Delonia.

The two sisters ran to the junction of the peach tree row and the daisy trail.

"Don't forget, Vendalia, we turn left here."

"I know, Delonia, we turn left after we cross the daisy trail."

"No," shouted Delonia, "we don't cross it. We turn left here."

"Don't get so upset, Delonia. Anyway, what difference could it make?"

"I don't know," whined Delonia, "but I don't want to take any chances. I think we should turn left here."

"I'll tell you what," Vendalia suggested. "You turn left here, and I will cross the daisy trail and turn left on the other side of it."

"Well, I don't like the idea, but I guess it's better than just standing here," complained Delonia.

Delonia started on her way and Vendalia crossed the daisy trail.

It wasn't very long before Delonia saw the orange tree and the banana tree. She was very relieved and wished that Vendalia had come with her. After putting the bowl, the spoon and the juice glass in their proper places, Delonia started calling loudly for her sister.

"Vendalia, Vendalia, where are you, Vendalia?" yelled Delonia.

"Hello," replied a familiar voice.

"Vendalia, is that you?" Delonia asked hopefully.

"No, it is I. . . Jasper, the green grass man."

"Oh, Jasper, I am so worried about Vendalia."

"Why, what happened? Where is she?" questioned Jasper.

"Instead of following the daisy trail on this side, with me, she crossed it to the other side," explained Delonia.

"Is that all?" Jasper said. "She'll be all right. It will just take her a little longer to get here. I'll stay and keep you company until she arrives."

"Thank you, Jasper, I'd like that."

Jasper and Delonia sat down on the grass and chatted about the day's happenings. Delonia told him about Sherman and his family. She told him about Felix the carrot, Madame Potato and Sir Onion. She also told him about her mother and how much she wanted to get home.

Although Vendalia still hadn't arrived, Delonia couldn't keep her eyes open any longer.

"Don't worry, Delonia," said Jasper. "Go ahead and close your eyes. I'll make sure Vendalia gets here."

And that is what Delonia did.

Suddenly another voice broke the silence. "Hey, sleepyheads! What are you going to do, sleep all day long?"

"Huh?" Delonia murmured, trying to wake up.

"Come on, get up. We have errands to do."

Delonia opened her blue eyes and exclaimed with astonishment and relief, "Mother, what are you doing here?"

"Well, I live here, silly," replied Mother while she gave Delonia a big hug.

"What's all the noise about?" questioned a sleepy voice.

"Vendalia, you're here, too," shouted Delonia. "I was so worried about you. Mother, you'll never guess where we have been!"

"Tell me about it over breakfast, sweetheart," Mother said. "Come on, Vendalia, it is time for you to get up, too."

Quickly and silently the two sisters brushed their teeth, washed their faces and got dressed.

When the two sisters arrived downstairs, Mother was in the kitchen preparing breakfast. Delonia asked excitedly, "Well, Mother, do you want me to tell you about our adventure?"

"What's this about our adventure, Delonia?" asked Vendalia.

"Well, you were there, too, Vendalia," insisted Delonia. "Don't you remember Madame Potato and Sherman and the green grass man and Felix the carrot and . . . ?"

"Oh, Delonia, you're so funny," interrupted Mother, smiling gently. "Now I suppose you are going to tell us that you met a talking tree, too."

"Yeah! How did you know?" asked Delonia.

"Really, Mother," said Vendalia, "you and Delonia sure have good imaginations."

Well then. How about you? Do you have a good imagination?

And one more thing. . .

Of whom is your tree more fond?

The End

Cee-Cee → 1976

Central Park Zoo
who taught me I was an animal person.
In fact I am a primates
PRIMATE

My elders! Especially Margaret Virginia
Dunn

AND SHERMAN DAVID LAKES,

They, espeially my Daddy
and lesser degree my Mommy (who danced
with Fred
(Astaire)
in Norwood
ohio
1946
1945? or 1947

Taught Me How
to BE a superb
Mother

180

Emmalee Vendalia Ballargeon ↓

All Three Sister? = Baillaegeon

Moie = Hez the Fez = Willoughbie Hannah Light = Gabrielle Adaire

181

SEEN ≠ Ker Local Media Ker Hand Delivered in Spring 2017

only NAMeS I Know

how can a TV station be

ABC - KNXV-TV, Channel 15
515 N 44th St
Phoenix, AZ 85008
(602) 273-1500
(CLOSED NOW)? what does that mean?

IS A LAKE
intimadated by the plural

totally Closed

NBC
200 East Van Buren
Phoenix, AZ 85004
Newsroom (602) 444-1212

Young wipper snapper snapper to send any thing it would just be thrown away

PSB - Also (Young wipper snapper Irving - Not to send

Why do

August 2019

FOX (KSAZ FOX 10 & KUTP My45)
511 W. Adams Street
Phoenix, AZ 85003
MAIN LINE: (602) 257-1234

Know of you learn About

potassium + how you could DIE

CBS 5
5555 N. 7th Ave
Phoenix, AZ 85013
602-207-3333

or
Robert Morris FREEDMAN
or
Tori Lakes - FREEDMAN

go ext lots of messages

torilakesfreedmanthegodmore@gmail.com ¡Feb.2017

een leaving messages for
to last night at KJAZZ

We even spoke after a baseball game 1993 1994 maybe 1994 possibly 1995

I'M CRUISIN' (IN MY CHEVY CRUZE)

Lyrics: Tori Lakes Freedman Music: Bob Frredman, ASCAP

makes you want to go While I'm

crus - in' in my chec - ro - let

spoken: 'Til I see ye next time, André!

No pints for the 'T', nothing hot and spicy
Corn fed beef with lovely tomatoes will be enough, you'll see
Now pick up the phone and gently hold it to your ear
Take a nap - the sounds that enter your ears are us saying we're here

Now let's gits makin' music
We make it every day
It's time to make music together
Ring, ring, 't'is I, got our passports. We're on our way.

Ye can naut kick The Rovers off the bus'
Ye can not kick the darlin' Irish off the bus
For they're our newest friendship
Ye can naut kick The Irish rovers off the bus

The Irish Rovers Management
Bill Girdwood, Booking/Production
~~Manage~~ Manager

1720 Cypress Point CT
Pahrump, NV 39048
Cell: 775-764-1371

No pints for the 'T', nothing hot and spicy
Corn fed beef with lovely tomatoes will be enough, you'll see
Now pick up the phone and gently hold it to your ear
Take a nap - the sounds that enter your ears are us saying we're here

Now let's gits makin' music
We make it every day
It's time to make music together
Ring, ring, 't'is I, got our passports. We're on our way.

Ye can naut kick The Rovers off the bus'
Ye can not kick the darlin' Irish off the bus
For they're our newest friendship
Ye can naut kick The Irish rovers off the bus

The Irish Rovers Management
Bill Girdwood, Booking/Production
~~Manage~~ Manager

1720 Cypress Point CT
Pahrump, NV 89048
Cell: 775-764-1371

188

Who or What
should we add to
this list? COX COMMUNITIONS →
other side
sue side

Apple Computer   Irritating
T-Mobile   oganizations

Nick's gang refused me attendance
   With Rabbi, priest, precher.
Told me I had no husband amongst
other AWLFUL threats, what they would
do to me once doctor's + staff of all
types had lessened do to time of Night.

sueable
Shammey Shammey Song
Earnhart Chevrolet
State of California
Banner Desert Hospital

Mentally
abused their
Dec. 2016

the
AIDE
Blue
smock
leader
is

N
I
C
K

Glass Magic
Professional Glassblowers

GlassMagicAZ/facebook.com
glassmagic__az/instagram.com
GlassMagicAz/etsy.com

Troy Kearns
520-270-6718

Paula Kearns
520-233-8945

Date _____			
M Glass Magic			
Address _____			
Reg. No.	Clerk	Account Forward	
1			
2			6
3			
4			
5	Stewart		14
6			
7			
8			
9	Colbert		
10			
11	To Jo Sullivan		
12	address		
13			
14			
15			

Your Account Stated to Date - If Error is Found, Return at Once

orange/Lime Green
on all

Date _____			
M _____			
Address _____			
Reg. No.	Clerk	Account Forward	
1			
2	Steven		12
3			
4	Colbert		14
5			
6			
7	Jimmy		10
8			
9	Fallon		12
10			
11			
12	Seth		8
13			
14	Meyers		12
15			

Your Account Stated to Date - If Error is Found, Return at Once

190

A ongoing list of the Shammey Shamey Song

_5 timer Alec Baldwin
3 " Woody Allen

- Sandra Bullock
- Salley Field (3 timer)
- Tina Fey
- Olympia Dukakis (3 timer)

Ellen = 5 timer

- Sheldon Blakely

_7 timer Jon Stewart & his little friend stevie
_5 timer Jimmy Fallon ★
" Tonight Show producers

- 2 timer: Seth Myers (New Hampshire Boy)

- Jeff Foxworthy
- Ron Wright
- Bill Engvil

R O O T S

- Mandy Patinkin - Nathan Lane - A&R Studios - Actor's Equity Very Rude
- Very sueable Phoenix Musicians Union = President Jerry Danato
- Edward Norton - Aretha Franklin (she & Doc Simon = good excuse. Returned unopened = Sorry JRT Jerry = Ben Still # Sweeny Todd S.S.
- Hal Prince -
- Robert Redford

TM, Kitt Williams: The man who got me Through 2015 → Sept 16, 2019 @ 1:51 Am

- Trevor Noah = Along with Comedy Central (five or six times (Trevor: son of Patricia) Was sent box with
3 filled pillow cases of Everybody stories: Het Patricia / Jon Legend Family

People I worked with or family member ... connection:
Ben Stiller   Michael Caine
Patti Lupone   Actually talked with several times Tom Conti

191

Bob Newhart — Bette Midler — William Morris Agency
(several times)
Harry Belafonte (several times) Quincey Jones of 125 E. 82nd
St.

SHELDON BLAKELY

Some go back to Jan 2017 (Most)

Next to THE CHURCH → 5 or 6 times

Crissey & Jon Legend (2 times)

James Goredon & Band plus

1 ⚠ **IMPORTANT!** Emily: ~~God~~ Goredon's
You must scan this alignment page for best print quality:

STEP 1: Lift the lid. Place this alignment page face down on the right
front corner of glass. Close the lid.

STEP 2: Press OK.

2

Production Secretary
this summer

192

SEEN + KER Local Media KER Hand Delivered in spring 2017

only NAMES I Know

ABC - KNXV-TV, Channel 15
515 N 44th St
Phoenix, AZ 85008
(602) 273-1500
(CLOSED NOW)? what does that mean?

how can a TV station be totally Closed

IS A LAKE intimadated by the plurel

NBC
200 East Van Buren
Phoenix, AZ 85004
Newsroom (602) 444-1212

PSB - Also (young wipper snapper to send any thing it would just be thrown away

Irving- Not to

August 2019

Why do

FOX (KSAZ FOX 10 & KUTP My45)
511 W. Adams Street
Phoenix, AZ 85003
MAIN LINE: (602) 257-1234

Know of you learn About DIE

potassium + how you could

CBS 5
5555 N. 7th Ave
Phoenix, AZ 85013
602-207-3333

OR
Robert Morris FREEDMAN
OR
Tori Lakes-FREEDMAN

torilakesfreedmanthegodmite@gmail.com

go nuts

est lots of messages

we even spoke after 1993

a baseball game 1994 possibly 1995

een leaving messages for

Feb. 2017

to last Night at KJAZZ

→ Margaret Virginia Dunn
March 21, 1930
in Cynthiana
Kentucky

Gilbert

Brentwood
New
Hampshire
space

Thank you, Rowbear — WHITE

Kellie Ward Burkhart

Andrew Lincoln Burkhart

Heather Diane Brillangeon

Michael Robert Brillangeon

Gabrielle Adaire Brillangeon

Emmalee Vendalia Brillangeon

Willoughbie Hannah Light Brillangeon

David Spencer Lakes Messer

Chief of Police – Lynn Haven Florida = David Spencer Lakes Messer

Rickey Earl + Jackie Kummer

Rickey Walter Kummer

Jack Kummer – very talented often imprisoned – drug + life
                    *Called Many times —— Tamela Lynn Kummer Bartlett

Earl Kummer *Called Many times — Tamela Lynn Kummer Bartlett + family
                                                                    Rodney
                                                                    Dustin
                                                                    Shannon
                                                                    etc.

Jack David Messer, George Ann Lakes,
...Kummer, Lisa + Terry Kummer, Jack David Messer,
Young, Douglas Kyle Young Doughy Roch Rhonda Kay Young Green, Robert
...lakes, Kathryn Victoria Lakes   Young Green, Robert

while an inmate in 2017.   in Palm Springs + the always ? Blythe CA.
                                        painted this for the love-of-my-life!
                                                            Rowbear

etline
Rodney
Dustin
Shannon
etc.

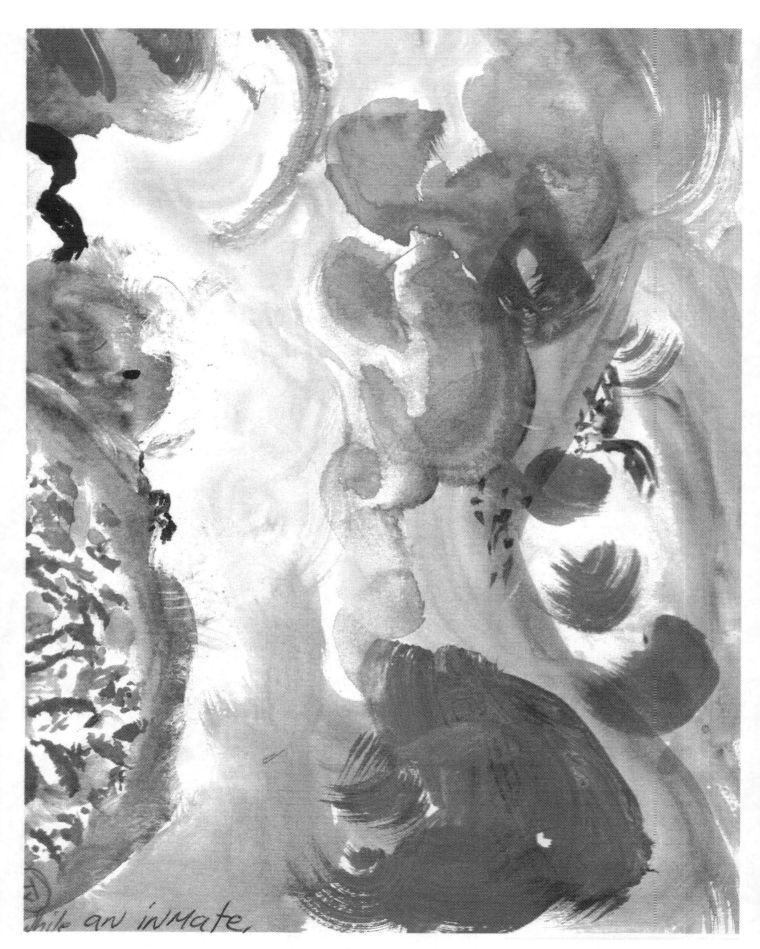

hile an inmate,

Moie = Hez the Fez = Willoughbie   Hannah Light = Gabrielle Adaire

Printed in the United States
By Bookmasters